SYMPATHY FOR
Wild Girls

SYMPATHY FOR
Wild Girls

STORIES

DEMREE McGHEE

THE FEMINIST PRESS
AT THE CITY UNIVERSITY OF NEW YORK
NEW YORK CITY

Published in 2025 by the Feminist Press
at the City University of New York
The Graduate Center
365 Fifth Avenue, Suite 5406
New York, NY 10016

feministpress.org

First Feminist Press edition 2025

Copyright © 2025 by Demree McGhee

All rights reserved.

 This book is made possible by the New York State Council on the Arts with the support of the Office of the Governor and the New York State Legislature.

 This book is supported in part by an award from the National Endowment for the Arts.

No part of this book may be reproduced, used, or stored in any information retrieval system or transmitted in any form or by any means, electronic, mechanical, photocopying, recording, or otherwise, without prior written permission from the Feminist Press at the City University of New York, except in the case of brief quotations embodied in critical articles and reviews.

First printing May 2025

Cover design by Dana Li
Text design by Drew Stevens

Library of Congress Cataloging-in-Publication Data

Names: McGhee, Demree, author.
Title: Sympathy for wild girls : stories / Demree McGhee.
Other titles: Sympathy for wild girls (Compilation)
Description: First Feminist Press edition. | New York City: The Feminist Press at the City University of New York, 2025.
Identifiers: LCCN 2024050153 (print) | LCCN 2024050154 (ebook) | ISBN 9781558613386 (paperback) | ISBN 9781558613379 (ebook)
Subjects: LCSH: Sexual minority women--Fiction. | Women, Black--Fiction. | Women--Fiction. | LCGFT: Short stories.
Classification: LCC PS3613.C4579 S96 2025 (print) | LCC PS3613.C4579 (ebook) | DDC 813/.6--dc23/eng/20241108
LC record available at https://lccn.loc.gov/2024050153
LC ebook record available at https://lccn.loc.gov/2024050154

PRINTED IN THE UNITED STATES OF AMERICA

Contents

- 1   Sympathy for Wild Girls
- 7   Throwing Up in a Gated Community
- 17   Scratching
- 31   Even Here, There I Am
- 47   Thinning
- 57   Exchange
- 81   Pollen
- 85   She Is Waiting
- 117   Nico and the Boys
- 123   Butterfruit
- 131   Be Good
- 167   Valerie
- 181   Swallow Worlds
- 187   Better Days
- 197   A Matter of Survival

- 207   Previous Publications
- 208   Acknowledgments

Sympathy for Wild Girls

THROUGH THE SLURRED lisp of her words, Daisy's mother whispers to her about dead girls. It starts off as a trickle of information, gossipy fascination over the feral, triggered by a story on the news or something that her mother heard on the radio while driving. But before Daisy can stop it, her mother bombards her with these stories every time she sees her, as if the presence of Daisy incites death. Normally Daisy can forget her mother's words. They're usually able to fall between her fingers and dry off in the light of day like water, but these words stick to her like sweetgum barbs, becoming more entangled in her hair and clothes as she struggles to pull them out.

There are girls whose bodies fit in the trunks of cars. There are girls whose limbs get cut up and stuffed in freezers. Girls whose bodies are eyed up by men even when they're cold. Girls whose final words are branded onto their foreheads like they're the only words they've ever spoken, used to rationalize their death, used to give reason to a killer. But Daisy cannot find any reason in bloated limbs that float down rivers or in the men who seek girls' bodies like flowers to yank from the ground, leaving behind crumbling dirt and mangled pale roots.

Her mother sees that she's worried. "You're pretty, so you'll be more of a target."

Daisy's mother tells her ways to stay safe, but they all come off as futile superstitions. Put your keys between your sweaty fingers, look over your shoulder, speak softly, move quietly, don't look men in the eye. Keep pepper spray in your backpack. Always tell friends where you're going. Stay where people can see you. Don't talk to strangers. Don't talk to men you've met. Be kind. Be cautious.

"When things happen to Black girls, they don't end up on the news."

The most important thing, her mother tells her, is to kick and scream. Don't go anywhere silent and gentle; leave marks, bite marks, claw marks, anything that can be evidence later.

At night, Daisy stares at the ceiling and shudders at the feeling of the sheets against her chest. Even through her pajamas, the feeling of her skin touching itself—her tongue dry in her mouth, her arm across her belly, her thighs pressing together—makes her stomach roil. She clambers out of bed, tripping against the sheets tangled around her feet, and stumbles into the bathroom.

On her knees, she thinks of every pair of eyes that could have ever possibly raked across her body. They appear to her in her dark bedroom, and she has no choice but to look back at them. She sees what they see, a small thing ready to be plucked.

She is trapped in her own body with no escape, no safety, no place to hide, not even the cover of her mother or her own good intentions. Her body no longer feels like hers. She is fat bright bait pierced against a hook, bobbing in the water, waiting for the inevitable. The sweat drips into the toilet bowl as she tries to heave out whatever it is inside her that turns men feral, makes them want to swallow her whole.

Then, in between her gasps, she hears the howling. Coyotes laughing, chilling and shrill. Chattering and cackling, louder and louder, until it feels as though they could be right behind her.

The noise fades away.

Daisy gets up and presses her sweaty forehead against her bedroom window to see if she can spot them. The only thing she sees is the sidewalk through the trees and her hot breath fogging up the glass.

DAISY DOESN'T COMB her hair for weeks. She lets her nails grow long, but because she is only thirteen they bend and break. They grow back in jagged and uneven, but she likes them that way. She showers as little as she can, only rubbing car air fresheners on her clothes when her mother complains about the smell. The stench of stale sweat rolls off her body when she moves, so the other children push their desks away from her, cross the street when they see her walking ahead of them. In part because of her smell and in part because of how she glares over her shoulder every few seconds whenever she's outside. At lunch she stays huddled in the middle of the quad, all her weight to the ground where everyone can see her. She stops speaking, instead choosing to communicate in settling looks, grunts, and, on one occasion with a boy who tugged at her matted hair, biting.

When she overhears the teachers entertaining the idea of calling her mother, Daisy knows it's time to leave.

On a clear, warm night, she takes her mother's coat

from her closet and walks right out the front door. The flickering lights from the television and her mother's snoring from the couch are the only witnesses to her escape.

She walks out past the rows of identical houses, green preened fields, plastic play structures.

Her bare feet slapping against the sidewalk is one of the only sounds at night. The other is the coyotes. She follows their laughing out into the edge of the hills, where her feet walk on top of wildflowers and tall grass growing from underneath rocks and pebbles, tumbleweeds and brush scratching against her coat. She slides down crumbling dirt and climbs up foothills, until their yipping is close enough to make the hair on her neck stand on end.

They emerge, slipping from the cracks and brush like shadows, their eyes flashing in the moonlight. There's six of them, edging closer until Daisy can see the full outline of their slender bodies, teeth bared. She swallows. While trying to calm her breath she drops her coat to reveal her body to the warm night air. The experience is thrilling at first, knowing there are no human eyes to watch her, to ogle at her, but the bliss is quickly quelled by the swipe of a coyote's claws against her thigh. Daisy buckles, but refuses to fall. She whines and turns to frantically look at the coyotes around her. They circle her, lunging to nip at her arms and legs before dodging out and rejoining their silky, turning carousel. *They're beautiful*, she thinks. The largest one there digs into her ribs. The pain shoots through her body, and she screams, the side of her torso throbbing and her ribs straining with every labored breath. As she cries out, the coyotes' swarming circle seems to falter, and so Daisy screams again, high-pitched croaking to a guttural moan. It echoes off the hills, splits the warm air into something bloodcurdling and cold. The coyotes back up, inky bodies moving into the ledges and cracks in the hills, until the biggest one's eyes gleam yellow and flicker out.

Their howls echo from their burrow, and Daisy lies back on the grass. She presses her tossed coat into her side and falls asleep to her fading breath.

DAISY DREAMS OF herself, seeping out into dry brush. The coyotes form around her, twisting around her heavy body, but instead of shadows they are light. Stars with cloudy tails spinning around her until they press their bodies into hers. Warm, soft, pulsing life covering her from all angles. They lap up the blood that blooms at her ankles and ribs. Tears well up in her eyes, and she realizes that she's found her place to exist. Here among fur and teeth and the dazzling moonlight: She will never be left to bleed out alone. There will never be any words used against her to try and explain why it made sense for her to die. She was meant for this, to stretch to the full extent of her limbs when she ran, to holler until her throat went raw, to lie down at night.

Throwing Up in a Gated Community

WHEN WE FIRST met as teenagers, Hillary told me that her mom wouldn't let her go near the apartment complex by our school because it housed drug addicts and thugs. I told her I lived there. *Do you know any drug dealers?* I didn't really. I had only ever smelled the skin of smoke at night as it haloed a stranger's bowed head on their shadowy balcony. But I didn't know if that counted or not, so I told her yes.

She asked me to show her around, and before school I woke up early to scrape the leaves and shining scraps of trash from the seams of the building. When Hillary stood there in her white sneakers—the thick soles platforming her above the ground—I fixated on the things her eyes drifted over. Beat-up shoes lined up outside a neighbor's door, the flies brewing in the heat of an entryway, a dog panting on someone's bare balcony. I concealed a mangled june beetle on the ground with my foot.

We passed a pack of boys doing tricks on their bikes over the speed bumps in the road. Management had made them taller after complaints about people driving too fast through the complex, and now you had to nearly come to a complete stop if you didn't want the bottom of your car to belly against the pavement.

They stopped when they saw Hillary. A shirtless boy with a bird chest rolled close to her, his body sun-blackened and musty with the odor of kitchen grease. It was the scent of cooking in a small space, when the entire home became an oven because there weren't enough windows for the ghost of your dinner to escape, leaving it to haunt the stitching of your clothes and summon a poltergeist of your sweat. Hillary tensed when he asked for her name.

I knew the boys. Sometimes they drank on our stairs, even though they lived on the other side of the apartment complex, so they wouldn't be caught by their mothers. My mom had stood out there one night brandishing a kitchen knife, our bug-misted porch light backlighting her like an angry god. She eventually let them stay as long as they threw away their bottles when they were done. I put my foot on his front wheel and rolled him away.

All the boys laughed behind us, but Hillary couldn't look up from the ground. She stayed wide-eyed, limbs tense, her red hair like paint dripping down her back. I led her out by the arm. The heat rose up from the pavement, but her skin was cold.

When we passed through the front entrance, she shivered back to movement and wrapped her arms around my neck, sighing into my ear. *Thank you*, she said, her voice shimmering in the heat.

I didn't hug her back. I was worried about what I smelled like.

She didn't ask to come to where I lived anymore. Instead she invited me to her house—a building tiered like a wedding cake. Her gated community was tucked behind a wall of cypresses hiding a circle of glittering sidewalks and pristine stretches of lush grass. A clear pond mirrored the sky in the center of it all, like a quivering glass egg.

Hillary's mother didn't work, but she had an office where she organized charity events and parties. Sometimes she'd wave me through her double doors, her phone tucked into her chest like a hiding bird, and ask me if I wanted to stay for dinner. I accepted the first time. They sat at a long table with place mats and forks laid out like rows of metal teeth. We had to put our phones away, and Hillary's mom reminded me to keep my elbows off the table. An older woman who cooked their food brought us our plates and drinks—I couldn't bring myself to look at her. Our hands were shadows against the white table, mine curled into each other like sleeping mice, and hers gesturing, giving. She took her plate into the next room, out of sight while her fork clinked against her plate. Hillary wouldn't stop talking about how I saved her from a group of boys. My throat walled itself shut as I tried to chew, and I mostly just pushed the food around my plate. The older woman took notice.

You didn't like it?

I told her I ate beforehand and asked if I could take it home. She placed it delicately into a plastic container for me. I emptied it into the trash when I got home.

Hillary's father asked me if I ever shot a gun. I told him no. He showed me how far his property stretched, how there were no fences keeping it in. He and his son liked to guard the crooked spine of trees that marked the end of their backyard and take shots at whatever crawled through. Hillary's brother was a pudgy middle school boy with a gold chain tucked into the crease of his sweaty neck, forever secretly trying to adjust himself in his pants. They would stand on their wraparound balcony with binoculars and shoot at whatever made the leaves rustle.

They once shot at the tail end of an animal, watching it yelp and scamper away, and drove out of their gates the next morning to find a coyote still against the road, entrails ribboning from its stomach. A little pellet from their pistol had been lodged into its throat. Another time, they shot at something that turned out to be a man. He had to be rushed to the hospital to stop the blood from fountaining from his thigh. Hillary's mom was mostly worried about getting noise complaints. Hillary didn't like it because sometimes her father and brother didn't go out to pick up the bodies of whatever they managed to shoot until the next day, and she had come across the stiff husks of raccoons, rabbits, and birds in the backyard before. The sight alone could make her vomit.

Hillary had a weak stomach, and a lot of things could make her throw up. Squirming things, squelching noises, and any smell too strong, from the scent of burnt sugar to shit. She inspected her food for signs of rot before she ate it and turned her nose into my jacket when we passed bodies of water harboring sea brine or pond scum.

Even her own body made her nauseous. She searched for shadows to cool under when we were outside so she wouldn't sweat, and she confessed that she always ran the water from the sink to mute the sound of her piss. When she told me that the sight of blood was enough to whisk the contents of her stomach to a peak, I asked her how she dealt with her period. She confessed that she didn't look, she blindly felt around her pussy to put in tampons and wrapped the used one in a tissue cocoon. She wouldn't look at her hands until she had washed them, and she held her breath the entire time. She told me she had learned to hold her breath for five minutes straight.

Sometimes I worried that she would sniff me out and one day she would hold her breath and turn away from me. I didn't tell her how sometimes our water pressure was so weak that the toilet could barely scarf down piss and tissue paper. I didn't tell her about the times I'd rolled up my sleeve and minced my own shit in the bowl with my hand. I didn't tell her how I wasn't allowed to turn the AC on in the summer and could spend the day marinating in my own sweat.

I didn't tell her about the trash bags and laundry that tiled up our walls because the trash can was on the other side of the complex and the price in our community laundry room had gone up by two quarters for both the washer and dryer, so we waited until we got permission from a family friend to borrow her machines. She lived an hour away, and in exchange for letting us wash our clothes there my mom would braid her hair and task me with babysitting her kids for the day. On the drive home, we'd stuff the car with laundry baskets and trash bags overflowing with our entire closet, and I'd sit in the back seat nestled between warmth and fabric softener, lulled to sleep by the rocking car.

I was worried that even without telling her these things Hillary would sense my lack and what spored from it. I only felt safe in the moments when garbage trucks or old people with strong perfume went past us and she tucked her face into my shoulder until I told her it was safe.

We both lived at home during college, which made me feel better about myself, even though the homes we stayed in were drastically different. If Hillary lived in my home, she'd probably find a way to leave. My mother saw me looking at college housing online and said it was white people's way to kick their kids out the second they turned eighteen. In exchange, their children threw their parents away to rot in old-folks' homes the second they became a burden. *But we don't do that*, she said.

Hillary didn't want to leave home because she didn't want to risk having a dirty roommate. She had binged dorm-room horror stories online and sent me videos of flooded staircases and students crowded six to a room, articles about stolen clothes and girls spitting in each other's toothpaste. She was happier alone, where she could keep herself and the square of her space clean.

It was that way of thinking that kept her from dating. Her mom asked her if she was a lesbian because Hillary kept turning down the eligible sons of women she met through PTA bake sales and charity auctions.

I asked her, *Are you a lesbian?* She said no. She said that she liked the idea of having a boyfriend, but the reality of one, having to fuck him or hold his clammy hand, grossed her out. She started dating Joel the summer before our senior year of college. He was a white boy with teeth that were crooked but bleached to the point of almost looking blue. He always joined her in the shade during her parents' Fourth of July barbecues. He once offered his jacket to her during a night when they were walking on campus together, and she told me that it smelled like nothing. Not sweat or cologne or even the overly sweet scent of fresh laundry. Just fresh absence. Instead of trying to hold her hand, he offered his elbow.

The night she first had sex with him, she called me as soon as he left.

He sweat so much, she said. His breath had fogged her windows and his sweat had laked around her naked body, saturating their outline into her sheets. She held her breath toward the end, in part because of the growing smell of his onion skin blooming under his armpits, in part because of the smell he churned in her own body—like the ocean in the morning. She told me how she arched her back to mimic his breathing, silent like the gills of a fish, and she didn't exhale until he finished, sighing in his ear.

He didn't seem to notice, she said.

Are you okay? I asked.

I'm fine, she said. *I think I just expected to be different afterwards.*

The question mingled in my head—What do you want to change? But I couldn't bring myself to ask because I was afraid of the answer. I didn't want anything to change. I wanted to stay in the static of her breath.

The boys on their bikes in my apartment complex had graduated to cars, rickety sun-bleached hoopties they stuffed all their friends in at night, doing donuts in elementary school parking lots, wearing down the rubber on their wheels while they raced through the streets.

They hollered at me when they saw me pulling out of the complex. *She's going to see her little girlfriend*, they'd say, and lay on their horn until I drove out of sight. I knew they were fucking with me, but I liked the idea that someone would look between me and Hillary and say she was mine.

I knew that I was only a guest in her home, but sometimes I allowed myself to imagine that what was hers was mine. I lounged out in her unmarred grass and pretended it was mine. I draped myself across her bed and pretended it was mine. When she smiled at me I pretended I was the only person she had ever smiled for.

I only allowed myself to think this way in between the

spaces of my own breathing. I tied these daydreams off at the ends so they couldn't sprawl into something that could choke me. I didn't expect that I would ever desire any more than what I got.

A couple months after she started dating Joel, I was waiting on Hillary's bed while she used the bathroom. The faucet ran the entire time. Then it stopped, and she poked her head out of the door, her face tight and eyes rimmed red. Her underwear sat crumpled on the floor behind her.

It's stuck, she whined, her voice thick with snot. *I was late but I assumed my period was coming. But nothing's there, and now it's just stuck.* Her shaking hand clenched the front of her skirt. She looked like her little brother adjusting his penis in his pants.

She told me she put a tampon in even though she wasn't on her period. She had left it in all afternoon, and now it was lodged inside her. It didn't have any blood to soak up, so it stuck to her insides, absorbing any moisture that could help slick it out. The feeling of the dry wad of cotton pulling on her sticky skin made her nauseous and panicky. If she tugged too hard she might turn her entire skin inside out, unraveling herself.

I didn't understand why she would put a tampon in without any sign of blood. It seemed like another marker of her cleanliness, that she would preemptively catch anything that could possibly stain her. My body didn't obey calendar days or however else people predicted the leaking of their bodies. My breasts could swell round and taut like grapefruit for weeks before my body bled in response.

Or I'd feel nothing for months, a drought for half the year, before my stomach lurched, clenched down like a bite, and birthed clots the size of my fists. All my jeans were thin in the crotch from scrubbing, all my panties were dyed with rust.

I didn't question her though, because she was crying. I told her I could pull it out for her, if the drag of her own skin was too much for her.

She splayed herself across her bed, her ass at the end of the mattress. I kneeled between her legs and dug the string out from the soft hinge of her thigh. I could see where the skin had plastered around the tampon corking her body, a lip-lock around a pearl. I peeled her skin away from the tampon and tugged gently.

You have to breathe, I said. *Otherwise, you'll pass out.* She folded her arms over her eyes and paced her breath like the tide. Beneath her hands, her face matched the color of her hair, while the rest of her heaving body paled into sea foam. The tampon stayed buoyed inside her, so I stuck my finger in my mouth and slipped it past her tacky skin, hooking the pearl out of her clamshell body. It glistened in my palm, as white and dry as bone.

Hillary curled on her side, sweat matting her hair to her forehead. She slotted her arm between her legs, like she was trying to tamp down something inside of her. Then she shot up and tried to snatch the tampon from my hand. I moved away instinctively, cupping my palm around it.

She watched me walk into the bathroom and wrap her tampon in toilet paper before placing it in the trash. She walked over to me with her head down and wrapped her arms around my neck. Her mouth touched the side of my cheek as a bead of sweat rolled down my temple. I felt her mouth kiss it away.

Thank you, she said against my ear.

Joel proposed to Hillary a month later. The diamond

ballooned on her finger like a gleaming wart, trapping all light and reflecting it back into my eye, piercing. We walked around the edges of the lake, stopping to watch our reflections waver alongside us. She said something to me but I didn't hear her. *What?*

As a trash truck rumbled behind us, I waited for her to tuck her face into my shoulder as it passed, but she curled in on herself, tucking her face into her knees, red hair peeking from her pale limbs like crab limbs from a shell.

She repeated herself, her voice muffled in the hollow of her chest.

I think you should stop coming over.

The reflection from her ring splintered from her finger, cross-sectioning her body with light.

I saw photos of her and Joel online a year later. Her skin blending with the fabric of a wedding dress, her and Joel's hands clasped over her belly, a pink baby swaddled in a basket in the same bedroom where I uncorked her body.

The boys in their cars saw me mourning on my balcony. They honked their horns at me until I looked up at them. One leaned out the passenger-side window. *Where's your girlfriend?*

I noosed my fingers around the throat of a bottle and flung it toward his car. The glass shattered and glittered down the rooftop, melting into the street like light confetti. The boys cursed at me, their wheels screeching as the bottom of their cars struck against the speed bump.

Porch lights flickered awake throughout the complex, wires humming to call the flies, singing and singeing, always returning.

Scratching

THE KIDS AT Calvin Village Elementary School made me feel better and worse about myself. I often thought about how every adult in my childhood had done me wrong and how angry that made me, but at least I didn't have it like the kids at Calvin Village. The last school nurse sent most of the kids home with notes saying they needed to be treated for ADHD. Just for doing things like interrupting their teachers or fidgeting in their seat—these dusty kids who couldn't afford breakfast, had no qualified teachers in their schools, and had the constant presence of the county prison looming from the horizon at all times.

She was actually fired after being caught handing a child pills without a prescription. Dropping them into a boy's open mouth and closing it with her hand, watching him fizzle out and droop against the hallway walls. He told his parents about the candy the nurse had given him to help him stay focused in class.

After she left, the kids were still either slushy and melting against their desks or running like little comets through the halls. I was hired as the replacement, with no qualifications or experience. I had an uncompleted bachelor's in nutrition, and the school said this was enough. They just needed someone to give out Band-Aids and ice packs like a normal school nurse would. Give them tissues to stop their nosebleeds. Little containers to carry their loose teeth home in. I just tried not to make them any worse.

Gertie was my favorite. She reminded me of myself as a kid. When I first started working there, she came in all the time during lunch. Other children would come in sniffling, sobbing while cradling whatever scrape or bump they had, guided by a teacher or a group of friends. But Gertie would just solemnly walk to the entrance and proclaim the problem, like a third-grade politician: *I scraped my knee. I have a bruise. My stomach hurts.* Then she'd sit and eat some loose fruit snacks from her pocket.

She was so stone faced, like a small adult. Even her name was tragically geriatric: Gertrude. I once tried calling her *Gert*, after feeling strange about the silence passing between us. She had snapped her head up to look at me and scowled. I understood immediately: there was no fixing the name Gertie in any way. Our relationship was conditional on the maturity between us both. She didn't want to be treated like a child.

I had gotten used to our meetings and looked forward to them. I started offering her a chair on the opposite side of my desk after I iced whatever scratch or bruise she had that day, and we ate while reading from the outdated medical journals my girlfriend Kelly subscribed to. She told me that I didn't need to read any of them to be a school nurse, but I liked to think that I could have absorbed something useful. Sometimes I would see Gertie try to rip out pages very quietly and fold them into her pockets, so at least she was getting something out of them.

One day she kicked the metal desk, and the noise made

SCRATCHING

me flinch. She watched me with her still face. "You wanna see something?"

"Sure," I shrugged, trying to find some line between caring, enthusiastic adult and casual colleague. She reached her hand into the pocket of her school uniform, and I noticed for the first time that it was dark and wet. She set it down on my desk: a limp brown mouse, with drying blood on its fur.

I knew Gertie wasn't shy around animals. Her father, Mr. Holt, had a farm, and a noisy sty of pigs that I saw when I drove to work each morning. An unspoken segregation cut through the town. My apartment with Kelly was on the nicer part of town—which just meant that the houses had a second floor and the patch of grass out front was actually green. On multiple occasions, some sugar-voiced pageant retiree had come up to me and blocked my way to my front door. *Now honey, where do you live?* And I would stand and find several different ways to say I lived on the second floor until Kelly came back home to let me in. The snorting signal of Gertie and her father's sty was a bittersweet signal that I had returned to where I belonged. Mr. Holt trained the piglets to race in order to take the fastest to the Oklahoma City State Fair, and I'd sometimes see him standing on one end of his field yelling to the piglets while Gertie held an apple skewered on a sharp stick, running over little dirt hills to lure them back to her father.

I liked Gertie for this reason as well: She was bullied. I don't think she was any poorer than most people in town, but she came to school dusty kneed and her plaits uneven.

Her perpetually sullen face didn't do anything to help her. She looked ready for a fight at all times. I liked the idea that I was a place of solace for her. And that someday when she thought of me, she'd credit me as the one grown-up who was looking out for her.

I had confided to Kelly about this indulgent daydream while resting my head in her lap.

"I'll have been the one who gave her a place to grow, you know?"

"I love you so much," she had said, "but don't count on it."

So, I smiled at Gertie, pointed at the little mouse, and asked her if she found it that way.

"Yes," she said, still analyzing my face.

"Wow," I said. "That's cool. That's so cool."

She nodded like I had passed a test, and I felt a rush. She scooped the dead mouse back into her pocket and leaned back in her chair with a medical magazine. There was a red smear mark on the table.

On the outside nothing changed. She didn't smile or become more talkative, and we were both still hiding away in the nurse's office. But now I felt like I had a clear purpose in my job, one that meant more than passing out bandages. I didn't tell anyone, not even Kelly, in part because I didn't want the illusion ruined—and I didn't want to lose Gertie's trust.

Every day, she showed me a new small dead thing: scorpions from her pocket, crushed hummingbirds found in bushes. And each time I couldn't wait to tell her how cool she was for showing these things to me.

SCRATCHING

KELLY DIED A few months into my routine with Gertie. She had been studying to be a nurse and was far more driven than I knew how to be. Being gay in that town was bad enough, but the friends who mustered up the courtesy to get to know Kelly's girlfriend always seemed ready to stage an intervention after knowing the different paths we were on. Or at least it felt like that to me. Kelly: soon to be a well-paid nurse. Crystal: lingering dropout, now working as an underfunded school's last resort. I couldn't really keep up with her, so I didn't try. I just stood by with hot coffee during her all-nighters.

She died in a fire at her college, the only one in town: an expensive private university to get these already poor kids to fall into the trap of debt. The lack of oxygen killed her, not the burning. Her parents wiped away the soot from her body and kept her on ice. They told everyone all about the chemicals that funeral homes pump into your family when they die, just to take your money. They thought human beings were too disconnected from death—human beings could not process and grieve the death of a loved one if someone was paid tens of thousands of dollars to make them look like they were still alive. They were hippy spiritual types. Wind chime types. Crystals lined up on their porch. It was warmer outside in the snow than in their house, where they sat around in sweaters and scarves, sipping hot tea with little flower petals floating on top.

The ice was packed underneath and around her body. Her skin was gray, and her folded hands still had black soot in the half-moons of her nails. I wanted to reach out and touch her forehead. It was the way her parents still talked about her. *Go ahead, Crystal, Kelly's waiting for you. Ooh, are these camellias? Kelly will love these. She loves these.* It kickstarted a little flutter in my chest and made me think that she was still alive, just very sick and waiting for me to wake her. But I knew that if I touched her skin, I'd want to throw up. So I just placed the little bouquets I got from the corner store in the Hobby Lobby parking lot on the coffee table and told myself that Kelly would probably be up the next time I saw her.

I DIDN'T TAKE any days off after Kelly died. I didn't even cry. Kelly's parents tried to encourage me to go home and rest—sent me off with a flask of tea that tasted like how sweaty feet smelled. But every time I tried to lie down, pressure gathered in the air and pressed down onto my chest. I sat up choking every few minutes, and when Monday came along I showed up to work just before the sun peeked over the horizon, when the sky pulsed violet. I passed Mr. Holt's farm. He was out front alone, kneeling in the sty with his pigs. He rose up from his knees holding one of the piglets. It was still and limp like rope in his arms. He stared at it, his body equally still and shoulders drawn up tight. The other piglets squealed around his ankles, snorting and puffing up fog from their warm snouts.

That day, Gertie dropped a dead lizard on my desk—a big blue lizard with half its tail cut off. I didn't know anything like that even lived in Oklahoma, but I was too slow to tell her I thought it was cool. Any words I could say were vomit building up in my throat. Gertie noticed.

"You don't like it."

"I like it," I croaked.

"You look sick."

This threw me off, and suddenly my face was hot. I didn't like the idea of seeming weak in front of her.

"I didn't get a lot of sleep is all." Then, out of fear of making Gertie feel as if I was keeping her in a child's place, I said, "Someone I know is sick. She's dying."

Gertie sat back in her seat, a pensive tilt to her head. It eased the weight of my shoulders a bit to see that I had said something that interested her, and I was about to ask her about her classes when she asked, "What are you going to do about it?"

"There isn't much to do about it."

"You're not even going to try?"

A pit burrowed in my stomach. "That isn't something you can do."

Gertie frowned and hopped out of her seat. I stood up, thinking she might leave, but she just crouched down near her backpack and fished out a crinkled medical magazine.

She spread it to a dog-eared page and turned it so I could see. "These guys are doing it, I think. So am I."

My eyes skimmed across the article, packed with a bunch of science jargon I couldn't really make out. There was a lot about pigs.

Gertie's words caught up with me.

"What exactly have you been doing?"

After school, Gertie took me to a twisted grove that led to her house. It was sparse, especially with the ice taking the place of leaves, but the black branches curled in around us like gnarled hands.

A ripped-up garbage bag sat tented up on the ground, and Gertie lifted it up to reveal three short planks of wood perched against each other. She took the wood down to display her collection: a few bent-up straws, a cut-off rubber hose, some exposed electrical wires, a pair of scissors, and the most recent dead animals that Gertie had shown me. The animals were black and stiff, dismembered, their stomachs and heads stuffed with straws and tubes.

I stumbled back and gagged, using my shirt to cover the smell of rot and also to wipe the sweat beading up on my burning skin. "Gertie, what the hell? Why are you keeping this here?"

She rushed to defend herself. "Because I can't keep it at home. My daddy wouldn't like it."

I tried to calm down, to get my stomach to stop flipping in on itself. I squatted down with my shirt still pulled over my face and picked out the loose wires with my finger. "Why this?"

"I was trying to put electricity in it." She pointed to a branch on a tree where some ruddy loose pieces of dental floss flittered in the air. "The article said it works better if they're upside down."

A fly twitched across the caved-in eye of a squirrel.

"Gertie, I'm not sure if any of this would work out. Those guys who did this had teams and like—a lab. Equipment."

"You could be my team."

My shirt fell from my face. I stared at her. "What?"

"You can help me—and maybe you can buy some of the things we need because you're an adult. And then maybe if we make one of the animals come back to life, we can keep your friend from dying."

"What makes you think I could do this?"

Gertie tilted her head to the side. "You can't?"

Something kicked up in my chest. I wanted to tell her no, I couldn't do whatever it was that she was asking me to do. But those words felt like some kind of magic spell, and saying them would break whatever powers led Gertie to believe that I was someone who could reverse death. The longer I let the question sit, the more confused I was by my own hesitation. Why couldn't I bring an animal back to life? Gertie thought I could do it. Of course I could help. I told her so. She simply nodded and began to cover her animals back up, and suddenly bringing a dead thing back to life felt like something I had been doing my whole life—as sure as breathing.

I SPENT THE night reading through that article. Looking back, it was extremely complex and involved a lot of expensive machinery I couldn't afford and would never be able to afford. The point was to get blood flowing back into a dead body again. Veins and capillaries shriveled up after death, like a dry river. The scientists in the article weren't even able to bring an animal back to life—not in any sort of Mary Shelley way. But they did get enough life back into the brain of a pig for it to be slightly alive. Slightly alive was better than completely dead.

We set up in my apartment. I didn't want anyone to see me kneeling in the woods with a child, playing with animal corpses. If you're thinking about how a child in my home looked much, much worse, you have to understand that our town was slow to catch up on the value of children's safety. I wrote a note saying I was Gertie's in-school tutor who was helping her with math. I gave it to Gertie to give to Mr. Holt, and she was at my place the next day.

"What did he say?"

Gertie shrugged and dropped her things down like she lived there. "He didn't really look at it. He's busy with the pigs."

After visiting Kelly, I would start the day by meeting Gertie on the other side of the woods. We'd wade through the red mud and find little animals. Sometimes Gertie would pop a bird with a stone, and sometimes I'd stick my hand down mice burrows or dive to snatch a lizard from underneath a rock. This impressed Gertie, so I made a point to do it every time we met up—I spent all our time together slathered in mud.

I hadn't slept since Kelly died, and I didn't sleep for an entire week while I helped Gertie. I survived on coffee, determination, and praise from Gertie. I hung rodents by their feet from wire hangers, sticking needles and tubes into their limp bodies, and she'd look up at me, dark eyes shining like a peering bird. I wanted to skin animals forever just to keep her looking up at me. I sliced the bellies of rats, and she held a bucket underneath to catch the blood. We cracked open woodpecker skulls, and I held sliced brains steady in my palm while guiding Gertie on getting the needle into a vein.

When she became cross-eyed and her hands were too shaky, I made her hot chocolate and she sat down in the hall to watch me work. We had to keep the apartment cold, so I wrapped her up in my scarf. She would fall asleep while I rinsed my hands off in the sink, watching the water run clear.

SCRATCHING

MY HEART FELL into this practice smoothly—visit Kelly, go to school, dismember animals at my apartment, and drive Gertie back home.

I had almost forgotten why we were doing all this.

A little more than a week after her death, Kelly's parents told me they were going to take her home.

I blinked at them.

"But—she is home."

"Oh, no sweetie," said her mother, "we mean her permanent home." She glanced up at the sky a little.

My mouth felt like drywall.

"How soon? You can't keep her a little longer?"

Her parents looked at each other. Sharing the same thought. "Well, Crystal, everyone's had a chance to say goodbye—and it's a lot of upkeep."

"Kelly?" I scoffed.

"Her body, sweetie."

I looked at Kelly, and it was as if the strange, bright tint that Gertie had put on my perception suddenly switched off. The black soot in her nails seemed starker, set in. As if it was a part of her now. Her face had started sinking.

I stormed out, sweaty and fuming. A week's worth of exhaustion piled onto my back, and the crushing feeling in my chest pressed down hard, leaving me gasping in the seat of my car, clenching the steering wheel with my clammy hands. I hated myself for looking like a child in front of Kelly's parents, I hated myself for not being fast enough for Kelly, and I hated myself for possibly failing Gertie. Failing her felt like death, and my thoughts hummed with all the ways I planned to keep myself alive.

GERTIE WAS OFF that same day. Instead of sitting in the nurse's office with her calm blank demeanor, she spent the whole lunch period looking like someone had pulled down hooks at the corners of her mouth. In my apartment she was more tense, her little shoulders hunched up and her face turning red in the center.

The animals that we kept in Tupperware and dog cages skittered against their containers. Her hands shook as she tried to guide a syringe in a bird's plucked neck. She kept poking it in the face, scratching it against the beak.

I tried to speak calmly to her, tried to guide her, but she threw the syringe down on the ground.

"It's fine," I said. "I can do it."

"They're too small," she huffed.

The veins of the bird. We were supposed to get blood flowing through capillaries, which we couldn't even see, and the veins of the little animals we had caught were still hair thin. I had tried something bigger this time: a crow I had hit with my car that morning.

"That's okay, we can just try something bigger—"

The words *next time* died on my lips. Kelly was being buried tomorrow. There was not going to be a next time, but the weight of that hadn't caught up with me yet. Not with Gertie around.

She began to cry, quiet and sniffling like she was trying to make the tears go backward.

Watching her cry was like watching a new car begin to break down, like watching an animal rot rapidly in front of your face. I kneeled down and tried to get her to stop. I stroked her hair and told her things were fine—*Don't cry, please stop crying.*

SCRATCHING

Her words whined from her mouth like a deflating balloon. "Hoover is dying."

"Hoover?"

"My pig," she sniffed, gasping between her words. "All the pigs are getting sick and dying, and Hoover is next."

I stared at her. "*Oh*, you and your daddy do those pig races. Are you upset because you can't join the state fair now?"

She stared at me blankly before shaking her head. "Hoover isn't a racing piglet. He's just mine."

I was so confused by her crying. I didn't see her as a child who could get upset about pigs dying. I didn't really see her as a child at all, so her crying felt more like a coworker suddenly breaking down during their shift about their pet possibly dying. It felt understandable but strange and inappropriate.

"I don't want to do this anymore," said Gertie.

"What? You can't stop. You're so close. We just need something bigger. I can get that for you."

"I want to be done, Miss Crystal."

"Gertie, you're giving up so easily." I kneeled down to face her, feeling frantic. "Great people in the world don't just give up after a *week*. Scientists and doctors and actors and anyone good at anything have to work for a long time. It takes months and years to get to something this great—and sometimes you don't even get to what you're reaching for. But I know *you* can."

She shrunk back, vanishing in front of my eyes. A small wet thing I could hold in my palm.

"Miss Crystal."

I took her cold hands in mine. "I can help you be great."

She looked down to the ground. "I don't want to." She tried to slip away.

"Gertie, *come on*," I pleaded.

She snatched her hands away from mine and fell back to the floor. I went to help her up, but she kicked me in the stomach. She kept kicking and screaming, knocking her fists against the ground.

All the animals in their cages flapped and thumped at the noise, shrieking and squeaking along with Gertie. The noise rose and wrapped itself around me, pulling tighter and tighter, and my chest closed in on itself.

Even Here, There I Am

THE SUMMER AFTER graduation I found out that my childhood friend believed she was a prophet. A professor that I had grown close to recommended me for a job in Berkeley, and I was staying with my grandmother in my hometown of Campbell, Oklahoma, for the summer before I could start working in the upcoming school year. She offered to let me stay even longer, but I was only there because I had no other options. I wanted to leave as soon as possible.

My grandmother didn't turn on the air conditioning between 2 p.m. and 9 p.m. because it cost too much money. All night and through the afternoon she kept the air on, cooling our joints stiff. Then at 2 p.m. she had us clench the blinds closed and flip off every light, leaving us thawing in the dark as the heat inevitably seeped through the seams of the walls and melted our bodies soft.

For the first couple of weeks I was determined to get through the summer with as little human interaction as possible. My bedroom was still decorated with all the old drawings I did when I still thought I wanted to be an artist. My shelves were packed with figurines from games I no longer played, decks of cards, hoards of empty glass bottles, a jar of paper stars, a single earring that I had made out of a paperclip, and a library card keychain. A plant on my desk that I had left thin and wilting four years ago was dark and lush.

I only came out of my bedroom when my grandmother told me to in order to meet with visiting relatives and neighbors who I hadn't seen since high school. They held my face, stroked my arms, and hugged me. *Do you remember me?* I said yes and let myself be hugged while I struggled to remember their names.

Otherwise I was in my room.

I'd lie on the floor underneath my window while the strip of light creeping from underneath the curtain seared across my face. I wanted to shut my eyes against the light and wake up in September, but I'd always find myself in the same place, the seconds solidified like the red clay in the punishing heat.

When I realized staying indoors all summer would cook me numb before I could leave, I tried imitating the schedule I had back at school: rising before the sun and trekking across campus for classes, walking back. In California, the ocean cooled the air early in the morning, offering gusts of relief from the heat. In Campbell, the relief had never been there. Any wind that cut through the curtain of heat was hot enough to cure my throat dry as I huffed in the sun-choked air. The sidewalk crumbled away beneath my step, and the sun seemed to take up the entire sky—glaring the endless stretches of yellow grass into panes of light, with only the thin strips of road splitting them apart.

At least when I was moving I felt like I was doing something, moving my way toward something. I didn't realize I was moving toward Janelly until I got too close.

About a month into my stay, I was walking toward the grocery store to grab something for my grandma, and I saw a small collection of people standing in the Rite Aid parking lot. Their voices carried across fading concrete, and the drivers around them honked and spit at their feet as they tried to maneuver around them.

She stood in the bed of a truck, the light from the sun behind her cutting her features to shadows. When she turned, I stood at the entrance of the shopping center in shock. Before I could move she caught my eye and seemed just as surprised as I did, before facing the sky and howling.

"And didn't I tell you? There she is—Nicole."

The girls surrounding her turned to me, staring as if I was a shining light. I only recognized two of them from high school—two white stringy-haired sisters with pockmarked faces. Their parents worked at the sex shop hidden away on Gore Boulevard. They used to trade bullet vibrators and lace thongs for cigarettes. Their uncle and grandpa both passed away from lung cancer, leading their mother to conduct random searches of their rooms and backpacks, pressing her nose to their clothes to make sure her daughters didn't tar their lungs useless. The girls would smoke at school, skipping class to hide away in the locker rooms, stripping naked and blowing air out the vents to keep the smell from stitching into their clothes. The others I had never met before—a big girl with bitten nails crossing her arms as she leaned against the truck where they stood, and a girl with black hair bleeding into bleached-yellow frayed ends.

Janelly stood swallowed in an Oklahoma Thunder jersey and gym shorts, her braided hair short and blunt just below her jaw. She hopped out of the truck bed, kicking up a cloud of dust, and stood to her full height, towering above me. I backed away as she reached to hold my hands.

"What are you talking about?"

The girl with the bleached hair spoke up, her voice tinged with awe. "Janelly told us you were coming back this summer. God told her so."

"You're going to lead us to our fate," said one of the sisters. "The girl tethered to nothing will lead us to finality."

"Stop," Janelly said gently. And the girls obeyed. "You'll scare her off." She looked at me with pity, and the spit gathered in my mouth like water against a dam. "It's been so long." She looked like she wanted to reach out and touch me again, but she stopped herself, squeezing her hands at her sides and then letting go. "How was wherever you ran off to?"

"California," I said. "It was great. How have you been?"

"Despite not seeing you for four years, I'm doing pretty well." There was no bite to her voice. She seemed genuinely happy, like a big puppy. "And can you believe I actually managed to find a calling out here?" She lifted her hands to the sky. "I have been convening with a higher power, one that told me to keep an eye out for you."

"Higher power? What, like God?"

"Yes," Janelly said. "Like that exactly."

I felt a deep sense of pity for Janelly and these girls. I glanced over at the grocery store, wondering how I could leave with the least amount of interaction as possible. The black-haired girl pointed at me before I could say anything else.

"Don't you look at us like that," she scowled. "Janelly is the real deal. She predicted Ceasar Jensen's house would catch on fire, and now it's all ashes."

"Once," said the other girl I didn't recognize, "Janelly said it would rain for three days straight, and then it did."

I couldn't help rolling my eyes. "Anyone can check the weather for the week."

"I also expected you to come back," Janelly offered.

"I'm actually only here for the summer," I said quickly, "and I'm pretty busy."

She gave me a funny look. "Doing what?"

"Getting ready for a job," I said curtly. "In California."

"I see," she said, nodding her head slowly. Then she shrugged her shoulders. "Well, a summer is plenty of time."

"For what?"

"To settle something with me."

I stared at her. "I don't know what you're talking about, actually." Then I shouldered past Janelly without saying goodbye. The girls picked up talking behind me, the chatter of their voices turning my thoughts to static.

They were still there when I left the shopping center. Janelly called out behind me. "Find me when you remember."

I did not look at her. I kept walking, the sound of the plastic bags in my hands whispering at my sides. I would not let her hook herself to me.

JANELLY AND I used to gamble with each other. Her mom would shepherd her to my grandma's house after school because she thought I could be a good influence on her. The only thing I had known about her before then was that in elementary school she used to be the girl who broke free of the playground during recess, and the teachers would have to run after her down the street to drag her back. She'd sit in class with the evidence of her escape etched into her body—the fence's bite carved into her arms, dust filmed over her hair. She never looked guilty, or even proud. Her eyes would flit around the room as if searching for the cracks in the walls, the thin spaces she could slip through. By high school, she had shaken her habit of running away, but she still could not root herself in anything. She was failing her classes, turning in blank sheets of paper for essays and quizzes. She had made varsity basketball as a freshman. I didn't know if she was actually good, even though she had the long sturdy body of a girl who was. But even this could not keep her steady, and the girls on the basketball team passed her by in the halls like they had never allowed her to jostle with them in their uniforms on the way to games.

I tried tutoring her in the beginning, tried to guide her eyes to my notes while she lay on her back in my room and picked at carpet fluff. Eventually she sighed and sat up. She took the pencil from my hand and finished the problem I was trying to solve, without any pause, showing all her work. Then she showed me another, and another, until she had finished my calculus homework. When I looked up from checking her work she smiled at me. For the first time I could see the pride on her face steady, like it had always been there. It gleamed from her and cut into me, her light tumbling down my throat until it rolled smooth and hard into the bottom of my stomach.

That night, I stayed up trying to think about what I had over her. The next time she stayed over I asked her if she wanted to play cards, since she wasn't going to do any work. She sat up eagerly.

"Is there anything you want if you win?" I asked her. She stared at me for a moment before looking around the room. She stood and grabbed a rubber band ball from my desk, bouncing it against the wall before saying that she wanted it.

I think I could have beaten Janelly without the extra cards in my lap, but all I did was solidify the inevitable. We played spoons, speed, slapjack, trash, poker, and sometimes just plain rock, paper, scissors. She managed to win sometimes and eventually won my rubber band ball, a DVD copy of *Monkeybone*, a pastel drawing of a farm I made when I was twelve, and half of a pair of earrings. From her I won three sparkly pens, her ticket to a concert in Oklahoma City, a glass vase that belonged to her mother that I had her smuggle to me, her old team hoodie, multiple sack lunches she had brought to my house, and $300 total.

I once beat her out of the sneakers on her feet. She didn't complain. She smiled when she said goodbye, and I watched her walk down the street in her socks, the dirt blushing her soles red.

I had lifted so much from her that she affixed herself to me. I guess she figured *I* was the one thing I couldn't take from her. She moored herself to my side and managed to drift toward me even in a crowd—even when I told her I was busy or hanging out with other people. *With what?* she'd ask. *With who?* She knew I was just as alone as she was. I was different from her though. People wanted to be friends with her. She had a bright smile and was easy to like when she wanted to be. I was alone because no one in my town had the same goals I did. No one else there craved excellence like I did.

At night, alone in my own bed, I could feel the graze of her hand against my knuckles when she took the cards from my hand. I felt the shadow of her body enshroud me. A tugging in my chest pulled at my skin as I tried to sleep. Once, I got up to follow the pull, walking barefoot through the night with a pair of scissors in my grip, ready to shear whatever was bound to me from the source. The bodies of resting cows and bison shadowed in the dark. Their breath mingling with mine—theirs slow and gentle, mine rasping in my chest. I walked until I approached the warped chain-link of a small house with a fenced-in porch, all bathed in yellow from the streetlight. Janelly stood on the porch in boxers and an oversized shirt, her nipples poking through the fabric. Her sweat-slicked face was twisted in confusion as she lifted her shaking hand up to the middle of her chest.

She took one step toward me, and I ran away. I didn't stop until I reached my grandmother's house, my legs pounded into jelly, curled in on myself in my bed, scratching at the soft parts of my underbelly—trying to carve out her hold in me.

We didn't talk about it again. During our senior year, I sat at my desk sweating over college applications while she lay down on my bedroom floor, watching a bootleg movie on her phone. She spoke without looking up at me.

"How far are you planning on going?"

"I don't know yet," I said. I didn't want to claim anything and have it turn out to not be true. "What about you?" We hadn't discussed college plans together, but I fully expected her to waste a few years at Cameron, a private university in the town that ate away student's financial aid money until they inevitably dropped out by their junior year.

"I didn't apply anywhere," said Janelly.

I went still.

"What the hell are you talking about?"

"My grades are trash," she said casually. "I don't even think I can graduate high school."

"Meet with your counselor then. You can still graduate."

Janelly scoffed. "I don't know who my counselor is." I could only stare at her. "Nicole, people from here don't really do much. I'm not going to school just to live in Campbell."

"Don't you want to be somewhere else? You don't want to live here the rest of your life."

Janelly shrugged. "I don't think I have much of a choice about that." She paused her movie. "People don't really leave here. Even the ones who work really hard end up back here sooner or later. I don't see the point in struggling so hard and getting my hopes up just to be pulled back where I started."

The silence pressed heavy onto my body. "I'm not going to end up back here," I said.

"I didn't say anything about you."

"But were you thinking about me?" I asked, my voice bitter. "When you think of some struggling hick, are you thinking about me?"

Janelly looked away for a moment, but when she spoke to me she looked me directly in the eye. "Sometimes it feels like you're from somewhere else."

"Not everyone is like you. Some people want to try in life."

"Yeah, but I've never seen someone try like you. You don't try like you hope you'll be able to leave, you act like you already have. Like you have no other choice but to not be here." Then, quietly, she said, "I'm jealous."

"Obviously not enough," I spat. For a second I thought I saw her confidence waver, and there was a softness in her face that I hadn't seen before, so gentle and open that my instinct was to apologize and end the conversation. Instead, I leaned in. "If you really wanted to leave, you'd do it. Nothing is keeping you here but your own laziness. You're not stupid, you could work to make some meaning of your life, but instead you're sitting here and giving up before you can even start. I'd rather kill myself than stay here. If you can't muster up the will to even finish high school, then you must *want* to be stuck here."

She was quiet for a moment. Then she laughed. "Maybe you're right. You're usually right." I had that feeling that she was looking down on me again.

After a moment of silence, she offered her fist to me from across the floor. "Can we play? Best of one?"

"For what?" I asked, my voice tight.

"If I win, you have to call me when you run away to wherever you're going. Once a month. Or at least send me letters. If you win, you don't have to."

"That's it? What makes you think I was planning on calling you at all?"

"Who else would you write to?"

I wanted to spit.

"I want your keychain," I said.

She pulled the little bauble from her keys—a plastic bracelet she had made herself out of candy wrappers—and set it between us.

I threw scissors. She threw rock.

EVEN HERE, THERE I AM

IT WAS WINDY the morning after my reunion with Janelly. Hot, dry, making the doors shift on their hinges and rattling against the windows until they creaked.

Most people stayed inside. I was out again. The weather reminded me of the Santa Ana winds in California, where the sun seemed to spur on the hot wind to keep everything at an angle. The normally crowded streets would suddenly empty, like a magic trick had cast me back into the lonely streets of Campbell. I would walk down the hilly sidewalks with no destination in mind, all by myself. In those moments, I could feel what Janelly left behind in me. Her faint latch in my chest would tug me in the other direction, so I walked in the direction of the wind to push me away.

Janelly was sitting at a park bench, beneath the black skeletons of two oak trees. The metal of the basketball hoop jangled in the wind. The play structures were rust-tinged and sun-faded. My grandmother had a picture of me as a baby at that playground, sitting at the bottom of a yellow slide that was white now.

Her hair rustled in the wind. She opened her arms to the air. "Do you see?"

"Sometimes it's windy, Janelly." I sat down next to her. "I want to get this over with," I said. She tilted her head at me. "I don't want to owe you anything. I want to make it up to you and then never speak to you again."

If I hurt her feelings, she didn't show it. She leaned forward on her elbows, and when she spoke, the roar of the wind muffled her voice so that I had to lean in a bit closer. "You took something from me. Unfairly."

I sighed. "I took a few things from you unfairly."

"No," she said. "Not something I can hold."

"What then?"

"I don't know. God just told me that you'll take something from each of us, and we'll get what we need from you."

Skepticism pricked at my nerves. I felt myself get ready to say something cruel again. If she was going to be a dropout, couldn't she have the decency to be ashamed of it like anyone else would be, instead of making up stories for attention? "How long have you been hearing things from God?"

"When you left, I waited for a letter or a call. After a year of waiting, I heard a voice in my daydreams telling me things that eventually came true. A building burning down, a dead dog at my doorstep. It told me that the fruit at the Discount Foods was going to rot overnight, and the next day I bought ten apples that were all black inside. At first the voice just felt like a feeling, like a memory of someone speaking. But after a while, the closer I listened, I realized that it was your voice. Even after a year I would recognize it anywhere. I felt silly, because of course it was. Who else would I hear?"

"I'm not God," I said. "I'm right here in front of you."

"No, I know it's not *you* you. But maybe God knew that if I was going to listen to any voice, it would be yours. When I think of a voice of authority, it's you. If you said it, it happened." A sick feeling rose in my stomach. *So why am I here?* I thought. *I told myself I wouldn't be back here, and I still am. What do I need to say to get the things I want?*

"What do I need to do then?"

"Come with me," she said.

She sat up and walked away from the park. I followed behind her. She told me about her disciples and how my voice had led her to them. Katherine, the granddaughter of the pastor of the Korean Baptist Church, who bleached the ends of her hair because she was too afraid of doing the whole thing. Janelly found her smashing the windows of the church late at night with a baseball bat. She was always halfway destroying things—just enough so that they could be fixed, patched up, or cut away. She wanted something to stick, a change she couldn't come back from.

Danielle, the big girl with bitten nails. Janelly found her on the ground covering her face while a pack of girls wailed on her in the dust. She was losing in a fight she didn't start. People assumed that she could fight because of how she looked, and when she proved to be soft, people used her to feel stronger themselves. Girls drove by her as she walked home and threw bottles at her back, boys felt up the part of her ass that hung off the back of chairs. Janelly was the first person to approach her with gentleness—to talk about daydreams and voices like memories. When Janelly stretched her hand toward her, it was not as a fist, but as an offering.

The sisters, Ebony and Cherie, had approached Janelly. They had heard about the voice of God Janelly claimed to hear. The girls, used to the uncertainty of smoke and their mother's anxiety, felt that Janelly's proof of God— the prophecies she heard and how they came true—was the most concrete example they had ever witnessed.

Janelly swung her leg over a fence to reach a barn—a squat brown building made of warped wooden slats with a roof that caved in like exhaling lungs. The girls stood in the doorway, each of them fidgeting with an anxious air. I realized in that moment that, followers or not, Janelly had managed to create a circle of people who wanted to be around her. I had never managed the same, no matter which state I was in.

I followed Janelly to the center of the barn, and the girls circled around us. Through the dim haze I noticed something different about the girls. They were all missing something. Janelly held her hand up to tell me to stay where I was before she walked around to each girl and collected the missing thing. Danielle gave one of her hands, Katherine offered an eye, and Ebony and Cherie both spilled all their teeth into Janelly's palms. Janelly walked back to me and gently placed the parts down on the ground between us.

"You know better than anyone about what it means to have someone give what they own to you," she said. She reached out toward me and stopped short of holding my hands. I bridged the gap between us and gripped onto her fingers as the cord in my chest pulled at my skin.

"Can you tell me," said Janelly, "is there anyone in California who you're connected to, the same way you are to me?"

The wind picked up, howling around the barn.

"No," I said. My voice sounded so small to me. "There's no one."

The two of us fell to our knees, not because we wanted to, but because it felt like it was what the other was doing. I remembered.

"Fish your confidence from me," I said. "You left it there, and now nothing else can pass."

"That's my fault?"

And I knew the answer was no, that if it wasn't Janelly, it would have been the light of someone else that lodged itself into my throat. Someone else's pride would pit my stomach, carve me thin-skinned.

"Yes," I said. "It's all your fault."

I closed my eyes and opened my mouth wide, and she peered down my throat. I heard her gasp, a gentle sound. The wind screeched high through the slats of the barn, rattling the planks so violently I expected the building to fall apart around us. She lifted her hand up and went to reach inside me, but the moment her fingers grazed my lips, the grip of her body on mine fell away.

I blinked and saw that all the girls and their parts were gone. Piles of red dust stood in their place. I reached out to touch the dust near my knees, but the wind scattered it away. It glided in the yellow fields and merged with the clay that coated the sides of the roads. As quickly as it took the girls away from me, the wind stopped and the air stood still, leaving me with nothing but dirt beneath my fingernails.

Thinning

I HAD BEEN wasting my time and money at an expensive gym for eight months before she started working there. An adolescence's worth of marinating in the internet told me that I should feel guilty for wanting to be thinner, so I convinced myself that my main reason for working out was to feel strong again. In high school, my body had been lean and sturdy from hours of sports—competitive soccer supplemented by school basketball during the offseason. I never appreciated how thin I was until I looked back on old photos taken when I was sixteen and realized that nothing about my body fit into the memory I had of myself. Not my face, now round and wide like a plate, and not my clothes—jeans carving ruts into my stomach, shirts choking off the circulation in my arms.

I couldn't walk up the three flights of stairs to my apartment without wringing my lungs weak, and while I used to be able to squat with nearly two hundred pounds on my back and run a mile in under six minutes, it was starting to feel like a feat to hold my body up straight for the duration of a television show.

Before Natalie, I had managed to get to a point where I felt healthy—where my limbs moved easier and I could walk to the grocery store down the street without needing to stop for a breath. I knew better than to check a scale. I knew how people got caught up in numbers. I had seen the gym rats track calories and grams and the circumferences of their arms to the point of breakdowns.

Those were all people with something to prove. They had to maintain their bodies to keep up with their effortlessly skinny friends or post muscle pics and weightlifting tutorials every other day to keep getting protein powder sponsorships. I didn't have anyone to impress, which briefly led me to believe that I was the only one at the gym for the right reasons. I didn't flaunt around in matching patterned two-pieces or scream and drop clanking weights on the ground for attention. Me, in my bleach-stained college hoodie and leggings, and the old woman doing fifteen pounds on the leg-extension machine were the only rational people in this expensive gym. Unlike the very people who worked there—toned bodies, bleached teeth, high ponytails, broad shoulders. They were always talking to each other, barely keeping an eye on who walked in and out, laughing when I scanned my little membership card and turned away. Why was I paying $59.99 a month if they weren't even checking? It felt like a dare—go ahead, we dare you, try and slip past us, as if we wouldn't notice a thing like you shambling in here.

It was the same with any beautiful person—which I had been sure that I wasn't since the first moment I was able to acknowledge my own reflection in a mirror—that I was invisible when I wanted to be seen and a light post when I wanted to go unnoticed.

When I first saw Natalie at the front desk, she immediately stood out from the other employees. Her hair was frizzy and unrefined past her shoulders, a cloud of fog, all of her cast in the same bronze color. Her features were delicate and full, like her face was put together from the shapes of rose petals. Her uniform shirt, which all the other girls tied or cut to expose their flat stomachs, hung low, past her hips, almost like a dress for her spindly legs to stretch from.

When I walked up, she kept eye contact with me, smiling gently. I scanned my membership card, looking down, and when it beeped she said thank you. Her voice was quiet but bright. I instantly wanted to hear it again. But the interaction was over. All I could do was nod my head and walk away.

The reality of my appearance snapped into focus. While I lifted weights and ran on the treadmill, I felt out of place in the gym in a way that I hadn't before. My legs felt bloated in my leggings, like two hams stuffed in fabric. My hair seemed flat and ratty, my hoodie too loose in the arms and too tight around my stomach—I was a Frankenstein of sweaty mismatched limbs. I wasn't above anything by dressing plainly. Natalie could pull that kind of thing off. Her lack of decoration made her look quaint and noble. She looked like the kind of girl a white boy would write songs about on his acoustic guitar. I was just a slob who had let herself go.

After my workout, I sat in the locker room, wasting time tapping my leg on the bench until there was a moment of silence, just me and the dripping shower heads. I stood on the scale and held my breath, as if that would make me lighter. The number flashed onto the dim green screen, and the weight of 208 pounds threatened to drag me beneath the ground.

Natalie told me to enjoy my day as I left. The shame of

my body muzzled me silent, so I could only wave behind me as I rushed out the door. 208. I knew how much I weighed in high school as an athlete, and now I had added over fifty pounds to that.

I didn't realize how small I actually was back then. I had been on teams with white girls whose limbs sprouted long and thin from their bodies. They all borrowed each other's shorts when they needed to—their skins so familiar to each other they could slip into them at will. They hiked their legs up on the benches in the locker rooms after games and made a competition out of circling their thighs with their hands, trying to make their thumbs and middle fingers touch. They would look in the mirrors with their shirts up and ghost their hands over their concave bellies, complaining about some excess I couldn't see. Their thinness felt innate, a birthright as girls who turned to light in the sun, and it was my fault that I wasn't skinny and never had been.

I was determined to be thin now, not just the way I was three years ago, but a better version of myself that had never existed. At home, I gouged my fridge of anything unhealthy. I planned my meals out for the next week, all fruits, vegetables, rice, and chicken. I even went out and bought a matching workout set, one that showed off my tits and hid my stomach. A sparkly pink thing that I tried on at home to just sit in, running my hands over the fabric until my palms were pumiced smooth.

At the gym I skipped weights and went straight to the treadmill, sprinting and jogging until the sweat rolled down my back. Growing up, my Aunt Talia religiously followed a regimen of Jenny Craig and Insanity workout videos, sweating in the living room in front of her boxy television. I'd peek at her from the next room, hiding because I knew if she found me, she'd make me do them with her, urging me to lift my arms higher, move my legs faster. She used to wipe the sweat collecting on her forehead and flick it at me—*When you sweat like that, that's the fat melting off.* I'd escape to the bathroom to scrub my face with hot water and hand soap because I was afraid that the fat she had flicked at me would harden onto my skin like candle wax, thickening my soft limbs. After working out I sat in the sauna—a corner in the locker room about the size of a closet—and steamed myself soft. My eyes heavy, my bones pliable, my skin flushed and leaking. I imagined the sweat gathering in a pool at my feet. I wanted physical evidence of my change, like those people in weight-loss commercials who demonstrated how they could stand in one leg of their old jeans. I wanted to wear old T-shirts as nightgowns and haunt who I used to be. But after each workout I found myself turning my body in the mirror and wondering if anything was even happening. The weeks churned on, but my body seemed stuck.

I disemboweled my fridge even further, consuming only liquids—soups, Jell-O, coffee. I prepared ice cubes for a snack, sucking until my mouth cooled numb. I made efforts to speak to Natalie more often—buying T-shirts and overpriced water bottles and energy bars from the front desk. Asking questions I already knew the answers to—What time do you close? Where can I get a towel? She answered my questions, she still said hello and thank you for coming, but each time she spoke to me a sense of emptiness barreled through my stomach. It's when I would realize how hungry

I was, how my joints ached and my muscles held stiff. What did I even want from her? The same finality I waited for in my own body. I wanted to walk in one day in my sparkly workout set and have changed so much that she had no choice but to notice. *Oh my god*, she would say, *you've changed so much!* And she'd wave her hand in front of my flat tummy and circle her fingers around my thigh, and it would fit.

The number on the scale dropped after I stopped eating solid food, and I spent the next two months in a lightheaded haze, twirling through the streets in tank tops and pants that were baggy around the waist. I didn't want to buy new clothes yet—I wanted people to see the evidence that I had been whittling away at myself. I didn't want a new wardrobe until my old clothes only functioned as parachutes, boat sails, curtains to gather wind, tents that could shelter anything but my body. My new body would not be kept hidden or gathered by anything—it would be a flag of desire staked into the ground, it would be a flashing hook caught in the eye of anyone who could see me.

This dream ended after the number slowed down, stuck at 153. It stayed there for a month, and I weeded out whatever food I thought was the culprit until I was down to water and vegetable broth. My body was still stuck.

I sat in the sauna on a day where the gym was mostly empty, my breathing warm and slow. The urge to quit nagged under the surface of my hunger, the idea slowly growing into a brightness that would have been so easy to fall into. I could leave right now, I thought, wave goodbye to Natalie and go have the things my body has been craving for months, dribbling burgers and loaded baked potatoes, comfortable clothes, someone to enjoy it all with. I hadn't eaten a meal in front of anyone since my first high school girlfriend.

She used to be leashed to the food she ate—a rope noosed at both ends. For her, food was not something to enjoy but an unfortunately necessary aspect of living, as clinical as sleeping or shitting. She kept a journal to track calories and planned meals a month out in advance, and she shunned me for snacking in front of her.

Do you ever think before you eat? Are you actually hungry or bored? I just want you to be healthy. And she'd kiss me, her mouth always tasing like the mints and gum she constantly kept in her mouth in lieu of eating. Sometimes, on dates, she'd take photos of me and delete them when she thought I couldn't see, so I began practicing being something she could look at and want to keep. I didn't eat around her, and at home I'd eat like I had to keep the inside of my mouth a secret, the brisk taste from her mouth diluted by whatever I was having for dinner.

I stuck my two fingers in my mouth to get that taste back, to purge my disloyalty to her desire, but the only taste in my mouth after would be bile and nickels.

It felt intimate even though I was alone, hitching my fingers down on the muscles of my throat, the bruises left on my knuckles after, my fingers slicked soft and bright. I thought it would be a change she could see, but she never seemed to notice. She just kept deleting my photos when I wasn't posed in the way she wanted, reigning over calories and the inches of her waist like a monarch of her body. So I gave up.

When we broke up, and when I realized I was no longer

under her eye, I swept the shelves of a gas station convenience store and filled two plastic bags with all the things I had stopped allowing myself to eat. I guzzled two-liter bottles of soda until it felt like my throat would split and ate chips and cookies until the roof of my mouth was shredded raw. I was disgusted at the strain on my body, at the acid burning in my throat. But lying there in the aftermath of my binging, I was awash with a sense of relief, like I had just awakened from the incorporeality of a nightmare and returned back into something solid.

My own breath circled in the hot air of the sauna, sticky and tasteless. My stomach echoed, as low and resonant as a gong. A wave of determination crashed over me. I tightened the towel around my chest, stuck my nails into my knees. I wasn't giving up this time.

I would excavate the weight from my body until the bones of my throat, my shoulders, my hips breached the surface of my skin. I would carve myself into something gorgeous from all angles. Slough away my excess until there was so much missing, people would yearn for my body instead of overlooking it like mountains and buildings, things people look past to find what they want. The room of the sauna suddenly glowed brighter, the hems of the walls expanding with light, loosening as the room began tilting, falling. My grip slipped against my own body, and my fingers slipped against the wooden seats as I tried to hold on before I fell, all my weight crashing through the ground.

My eyes opened to the white walls of the locker room, the cold air lapping at my sweat-soaked skin. Two employees stood over me, one making a frantic phone call and the other trying to force a water bottle into my hands. Another employee held my head in her lap, stroking my damp hair away from my face. Natalie. Her frizzy hair and pale skin catching the light.

"Oh my god," she said. "Are you okay?"

I wanted to cover my face. I wasn't ready to be seen yet. The softness of my body seemed to billow around me like something I could sink into. I couldn't speak. I could only cry, the salt leaking into my mouth.

"Aw," she said, putting her hand on my back to sit me up. "Here, let's get you something to eat."

Exchange

AFTER A MONTH of dating, my boyfriend Mark and I had gone to the grocery store together for the first time. I had made a show of palming a four-pack of gum off the shelf and into my pocket—squeezing his arm linked with mine, smiling up at him. He had stared at me, and I waited for him to decide if he would look down on me for it. The reactions of other guys I had dated had always been mixed. Some boys were wary and standoffish afterward, like this was evidence of something more unhinged in me—a fraying rope they were looking to let go of before it snapped. Other boys had the opposite reaction. Taking makeup from a CVS made me into some kind of bad girl, and I was someone they could press their dick against in public but still take home to their mother later.

Mark had grinned back at me, took my hand, and walked out of the grocery store without paying. No one tried to stop us.

Mark stood tall and bulky with muscle. Blond hair hung limp against his forehead. Squinting blue eyes in a tan face—one of those white boys who looked like the sun had met with the water and given birth to bleached, bright children. It was a point of pride for him.

"I look like I'm from here, right, babe? You'd never be able to tell the difference between me and a beach native."

When we were alone together, his voice naturally

pitched high and tight into a Midwestern accent. Like when I was helping him bleach his hair or counting reps for him while he did pull-ups from a bar he installed above our bedroom door. He only felt comfortable doing these things around me, but sometimes I'd mess up and forget to start a timer for his hair or lose count of how many sets he had already done, and he would complain about how I was trying to ruin his career.

The first of those careers: acting. I had an admiration for aspiring actors. Los Angeles teemed with them. I liked how they all came from different backgrounds, and despite how varied they could be, they all seemed obsessive. They kept themselves busy looking for work, practicing for work— whether or not they got it. And when they did, every actor I knew went through ritualistic lengths in order to transform themselves for a role, even if it was something nondescript, like a ten-second spot in a pizza-roll commercial.

It's part of what first attracted me to Mark. He was so handsome and simple; I was shocked to think that he possessed a quality that I felt actors naturally possessed: a desire to transform. What could such a beautiful boy wish to change into?

Nothing, I realized with Mark.

He didn't search for any auditions, and when he did have auditions, he showed up late and unprepared. Or he was too prideful. He couldn't bring himself to do any more commercials after watching his spot for a dog food advertisement where a border collie and stock footage of a wolf had more screen time than him. Then he was a model who was too stiff to pose. A lifeguard and a Little League coach who couldn't stand kids. Hand model. Foot model. Body double. I rubbed hot sauce on his cuticles to try and curb his nail-biting habit and rubbed his back when he cried about feeling fetishized behind a camera. Finally, Mark had a brief and tortured month where he considered an offer to do porn but ultimately gave up on that career path after deciding that he didn't want me to have to suffer from the knowledge that he was having sex with other women—a concern I didn't have and had never brought up.

I hated his Midwestern accent, not for the accent itself, but because it reminded me how Mark couldn't commit to one act. It also made me think of his mother, who habitually came over to the apartment Mark and I shared together, unannounced. She would rearrange our cabinets and drawers, take out the trash, wash Mark's clothes. We kept both of our dirty laundry in the same place, but she separated my clothes from his and left them at the bottom of the hamper. She would always argue with Mark but find a way to bring the argument back to me.

"You're never around to act as the woman of the house. You're lucky I'm here to keep this place looking decent. What do you even do all day?"

"I'm at school, or work," I said, looking pointedly at Mark. "If I don't work, we don't have a place to keep clean or dirty."

I had given up on trying to be nice to Mark's mother, and the sight of her alone drained me. I set my computer up at the kitchen table and let the two of them argue over my head.

"Mom, Quinn's busy."

"Oh? Well, maybe Quinn is just too busy to be your girlfriend then."

"Mom, come on."

"You were there for her when she was going through it."

Going through it: failing most of my classes senior year and having to pay for another two semesters of college.

"And she can't wash a dish to save her life. I swear, Mark, I sit at home sweating thinking about the ketchup caking up on your plates. Or the little rust spots on your spoons—if you don't get to that now, you're going to be hurting later."

"Mom," Mark snapped. "You don't have to be here then." I looked up at him, quietly stunned for a moment. "Quinn is almost done with school anyway."

MARK'S MOST RECENT job was working as a figure model for a local art college. He was only required to stand still and not look nervous freshmen in the eye while he was naked.

"It's hard work," he explained to me while eyeing the shelves in the men's shower section, "thinking of different poses and stuff. Sometimes I have to think of a different pose like every five minutes."

He dropped a bottle of shampoo into the shopping basket on his arm, and in the same movement, tucked a tub of mousse into his hoodie pocket.

Mark believed we had a right to steal, because we were struggling—despite the fact that I was the only one working. I didn't think very politically about it until my senior year of college. Up until then, I assumed no one would miss the absence of a lip balm. Now I wanted someone to notice.

We split up, and I shuffled through the aisles of Target in Mark's sweats and jean jacket—the pants rolled up on my hips five times and the jacket engulfing my shoulders. By the time I met up with Mark I was weighed down by copper salt and pepper shakers, sleeping pills, a pair of earrings, a cropped T-shirt, a DVD copy of *The Haunted Mansion*, and finally a tube of dark purple lipstick—because I had never tried that shade before. When we got home we spilled everything out onto the bed.

Mark had stolen a pack of skinny batteries, condoms, mousse, a big bag of mixed candy, an eight-pack of 5-hour ENERGY, and a box of super-absorbent tampons, which I did not use. He handed me the box with a big smile on his face.

I pulled my new shirt over my head and placed my hands on my exposed stomach. I leaned over to kiss him and left a purple tint on his lip, like a bruise. Then we watched the movie on the box television we had sitting on cinder blocks and wood planks. We sat side by side—Mark's big body slumped down, his weight shifting the bed, making my body tilt toward him. I sat up straight and kept a sliver of space between us, so only the heat of our bodies ghosted against each other. I liked the movie just fine, but I kept on getting distracted by the shadows and backgrounds. The reflection of my hair—short and curling around my neck—meshed with the black transitions between scenes, so for brief moments only my stony face haunted the screen, stark like a face rising out of a lake.

I THOUGHT MARK was too big to get away with shoplifting, but he showed me that the number one thing you had to do to get away with stealing was to do it with confidence. No stalling or stalking down the aisles. No looking over your shoulder. Most people, if given the chance, wanted to ignore you.

I BARELY NOTICED her. I didn't realize she was an employee when I first saw her. Her blond hair was stuffed into the back of a black hoodie, and she stood hunched over a cart while scrolling on her phone. I said excuse me as I brushed against her for a bag of cough drops, and she noiselessly leaned out of the way without looking up at me. I slipped the cough drops in my pocket as I turned the corner.

I paid for a Toblerone and a Red Bull before meeting Mark outside. He also had an energy drink in his hand, and he lifted it up to mine, smiling.

"We had the same idea," he said. "I got it for you. You seem to like this better than coffee these days."

A thank you teetered on the edge of my mouth as we walked to my car, but instead I said, "I feel like they work better, but I don't know. I might just be imagining it."

Mark looked ready to say something when the girl called out to us from across the street.

"Excuse me!"

We waited for her to jog up to us, squinting to see if she looked familiar, when I noticed two things at once: the first was that she was the girl I had passed in the store, and the second was that she wore a round name tag pinned to her chest.

My hand flailed against Mark's arm, trying to guide him more quickly to the car, but he grabbed my hand and stood still, smiling brightly at the girl. "Is there a problem?"

The girl stopped in front of us and took a second to catch her breath. A walkie-talkie beeped at her hip.

EXCHANGE

"I don't want to be nosy or anything, but I've watched the two of you steal from this store for, like, the past year. And you've never been stopped before."

My nails dug into Mark's hand reflexively.

"I think you've got the wrong people," he said. He reached into his pocket and pulled out a receipt. "We went through self-checkout. Here's our receipt."

The girl shook her head. The ends of her hair feathered across the top of her name tag: HELLO MY NAME IS SHELLY.

"I saw you," she said. "I've seen you." She pointed at me. "I saw her, just now. She tucked a bag into her pocket. And something else into her jacket sleeve before she left." A smile stretched across her face. "And I bet if I called security out here, they'd find something on both of you."

Mark's smile fell a bit, and the girl laughed—easy, bubbly. "That's not what I want, though." She glanced around, settling herself, and a creeping dread gripped me while I tried to find what she was searching for. Then she looked past Mark to look me directly in the eye. "Could I take you guys out to lunch?"

I SAID YES because I assumed we were caught and I was ready to give up. We sat in the booth of a diner across the street, and on the walk over I kept waiting for the bust. This girl would lead us to a crowd of cops who had been watching us steal from this shopping center for the past year, and we would be forced to pay back the full amount of everything we'd taken. Mark put his hand on my back as he sat across from Shelly, and I frantically added up the cost of every T-shirt, toothbrush, pack of gum, box of tampons, and frozen pack of vegetables—the thaw always numbing my arm and seeping through the sleeve of my jacket. The total price swelled in my head.

Then I stopped. I would probably just go to jail.

Mark gave me an uneasy look. "Hey," he said to Shelly, "we don't need to go through the charade of all this. If something is happening, can you just tell us?"

Shelly cocked her shoulder to the side, her eyes bright. "What's happening?"

Mark gave her nothing.

She sighed and put her hands up. "You can relax. I'm not trying to get you arrested. I'm trying to learn."

I felt Mark's eyes on me, trying to gauge what to say next, but I was too busy steeling myself for something to end.

"Learn what?"

"About how you walk into the same place over and over again and take exactly what you want and never get caught." She waved her hand in front of her face. "Forget not being caught. You two seem so gutsy. How are you not afraid of being caught?"

Mark chuckled, and my eyes twitched toward him.

"It's not that hard," he said, looking bashful. His hair looked yellow under the diner lamps, and I could see the splotches on his neck from where I hadn't rubbed in his fake tanner well enough.

"People who get caught are bad actors. They're looking over their shoulders and running out of the store. Good acting is about subtleties. Luckily I'm a good actor."

"Are you really an actor?" she asked, in a childish awe.

EXCHANGE

Her eyes were a startling blue—the ocean at midday. I had spent so long listening to Mark try and convince me how all-American beach boy he was, but he seemed ruddy and clumsy next to this girl. She had what he wanted—an effortless shine, an easy beauty.

"Yes," he said, at the same time that I said, "He used to be." Mark's hand slipped from my back.

"Wow," Shelly gushed. She leaned forward. "Is there any trick to it?"

"You just have to seem boring. You could wear baggy clothes. Nothing too noticeable, obviously. Sweatpants. A hoodie."

The two of them ordered burgers and fries, the latter growing cold and stale as Mark told Shelly all about how he learned sleight of hand from a professional pickpocket on the set of a television show where he was an extra and how he learned to keep a scene going from improv classes he took at the community center. He said the gaps where we hesitate is when the audience knows something is wrong. The entire time Shelly nodded her head and replied in all the right spaces. I didn't bother nodding when he went on long tangents like this—I figured he liked hearing himself speak—but each time she responded, Mark grew taller in his seat, preening and leaning forward to answer her, like she was a child.

"What about when you steal something bigger?" Shelly asked.

"We don't really take big things."

"Valuable things?"

"I'm sorry," I cut in, "but why are you asking?"

Her eyes settled on me in a way that made my skin

itch. "It seems like a waste of talent to not go for something bigger."

Mark beamed at the word *talent*. "Well," he said, "what would you consider valuable?"

Shelly turned to me and snatched my hands up from across the table. When she spoke, she looked me directly me in the eye, as if Mark wasn't there.

"I'm just saying if it were me, I'd want my boyfriend to get me something nice. He's never swiped you any jewelry?"

I shook my head. She stayed looking at me for a moment, and I kept her gaze, only because I figured that's what people who looked at others in the eye wanted. She suddenly clicked her teeth and shook her head, like she was saying *What a shame*. Then her eyes shifted to my wrists, and she gasped.

"You're so thin!" She examined my wrist in her hand. A red beaded bracelet circled her own. Without letting me go she pushed her bracelet down her own wrist and over my hand, pulled taut so that the red beads all gathered together at the bottom of the string, until it swished over my knuckles and gathered again at my wrist, limp.

"Keep this," she smiled, "until this guy gets you something nice."

She finally let me go, and the heat of her hand lingered against mine. "I want to help," she said. "I want to take something worthwhile."

I HAD ASSUMED Shelly was an underachiever, since she was so enthusiastic to slack off with strangers. But she told us she had graduated from the Academy of Our Mystical

EXCHANGE

Rose, an affluent all-girls Catholic school, two summers ago and was finishing up her second year of college studying biology.

Mark had asked, "Oh, are you like super passionate about animals or something?"

He had never gone to college, and his main references for why someone would go was me. When we first met I told Mark that I studied social welfare because I wanted to help as many people as possible. Because I desired to understand others.

Shelly said, "It's just one of the only subjects I was good at."

I spent a night looking her up online, hunched over my laptop in the dark while scrolling through school interviews, photos, and posts. Shelly holding a trophy above her head, Shelly rustling pom-poms on loop, Shelly in a debate-club blazer, Shelly shrouded in blue ribbons. The last photo she had posted was of her in a purple cap and gown two years back, standing on a podium with her hands outstretched toward all her classmates.

Shelly asked us out to eat multiple times after that. She talked less about shoplifting and more about Mark. I think she picked up on how easy it was to talk to him—he would talk about himself for hours when I let him. Sometimes it was comforting to start Mark's mouth like a car engine and know it would keep going. I would rest my head in his lap and fall asleep to the hum of that motor, grateful to forget that I was a person for a while.

I wasn't able to fall asleep at the dinner table, so instead I'd pick a spot across the room and stare at it or pretend to watch football on the television above the bar. Sometimes

I'd accidentally find my eye wandering toward her, until she smiled back at me, and I'd stare at my hands in my lap—her bracelet on my wrist.

I shut down most of the questions she asked me about myself.

Quinn, what's your favorite place to eat? Anywhere is fine.

Quinn, what's your family like? There's not much to say about them.

Quinn, why did you take a break from school? A wave of my hand—flagging down the waiter for another coffee.

She didn't mind my short answers. She reminded me of Mark in that way—she could make do with someone to talk at rather than talk with. When we left the restaurant, Mark would offer to go get the car and drive it to us so we didn't have to walk too far, something he had never done for me when it was just the two of us. In that time alone together, Shelly would hook her arm in mine and press against me, her breath warm against my ear, forming little clouds around my neck in the cold night, and she'd suddenly have so many things to say to me, without needing any answer. As if her words had gathered in her mouth and she needed to spit them all out in the time it took for Mark to come around with the car.

"You know, I know you didn't really have an opinion on it, but I think you would like the movie *Orlando*, you look like the main girl. What's her name? Tilda Swinton? You remind me of her, but if she was Black, of course. You know, my mom used to tell me that eating sweet things all the time means you're a bitter person, and eating bitter things all the time means you're sweet, and all I ever see you have at dinner is plain black coffee. So you must be a very sweet person."

I started looking forward to these little moments when someone ran to me and only paid attention to me—and I knew each one would only last two minutes. I could handle these small spurts of devotion if I knew it only had to last for as long as it took Mark to get the car.

We had gone dutch the first time, but Mark started covering the check after that. He didn't pay rent and was only responsible for a $150 internet bill once a month, but I was still impressed. He had never done that when it was just the two of us. With Shelly around, Mark would snatch the check away before she could slide her card from her wallet, and she always made a show of that too.

"I haven't quit my job yet," she'd say. But Mark would shoo us off and pay for Shelly's steak and potatoes and peas and large shake. My coffee. His soup and crackers.

He began inviting her over, with my opinion on the matter being a second thought. They'd start cooking together, which was also something Mark never did. He ate out or brought us meals his mom made—which I rarely ate anyway because I was sure she purposely put fat strips of uncooked onions and bell peppers and half cloves of garlic in her cooking to spite me, since she had asked me on more than one occasion what my least favorite foods were. Shelly asked me what I liked to eat, and when I couldn't really give her an answer longer than *Oh, I don't eat much*, she weaseled out what I could stomach through a combination of asking Mark and knowing what people who didn't eat would eat.

At the end of a long day at school or work, I'd come

home to find Shelly and Mark standing in our tiny kitchen, bathed in the orange stove light, craned over a pot of vegetable broth bobbing with cut carrots and mushrooms. Thin slices of handmade bread that cracked and split soft. Mark took my backpack or my jacket and told me to go shower, and when I got back, he'd be pouring me coffee while Shelly made me a serving of soup. She bought new bowls and plates—that only I ever used—small bright plastic, for a child-sized stomach.

They sat at the dinner table and talked while I did homework—Mark across the table, his legs encasing mine, Shelly next to me, her foot propped against the leg of my chair, slipping against my ankle every now and again. They'd stop after an hour and ask me if they were too loud, but I liked having them near me. I liked going home to two people happy to see me—waiting for me. Their voices hummed together, their spine.

I liked who Mark was when he was around her. I liked that he opened doors, and paid the check, and cleaned up after himself. The opposing parts of him that I liked and the parts I couldn't stand finally seemed to mesh back together into a person I looked forward to seeing at the end of the day. The two of them hung out alone together while I was away, and they let me know when they were going grocery shopping or planning to see a movie. I told a coworker about this while we stood behind the restaurant on our break. She and others would smoke out back, and I just wanted an excuse to inhale the fumes. It was an understanding we had that she needed to smoke and I needed to siphon this slow decay from someone else because I was too nervous to do so myself.

EXCHANGE

"Oh, baby," she said, "you know he's fucking her, right?"

I wasn't stupid—I suspected something like that was happening. I didn't expect a boy to be that nice to a girl he didn't know without wanting to have sex with her. But Mark's new attitude stuck even when Shelly was gone. He still made me coffee and brought me the four-pack of gum I liked to hoard from the store. He had even met Shelly's challenge to get me something nice.

He'd slid a little box across the kitchen table one night, when it was just the two of us. I expected something cheap-looking, or a joke gift, but when I opened it, a thin gold chain with a circular pendant gleamed back at me, my initial carved into its surface.

"How did you get this?" I asked.

He smiled. "Don't worry about that."

He stood to clasp it around my neck—his big hands fumbling with the small chain. When he stood in front of me again, his big shoulders hunched forward. His feet scuffed against the floor.

"Do you like it?" he asked.

I looked in the mirror. The pendant rested gently in the pocket of my throat.

"I love it," I told him. And that night, while he slept next to me, I turned the necklace over in the lamplight, trying to guess how he snatched it, trying to see if it was fake.

Shelly noticed the necklace the next time she saw me.

"Oh, Quinny," she said, almost breathless. "That's gorgeous."

I clammed up when she noticed—I was worried she would ask for her bracelet back. I had grown so used to its weight—rolling the beads across my wrist, swirling it around my finger or tugging it between my teeth when I felt anxious. My eyes flickered down to my hand, and she met my gaze there. Then she moved on. She never brought up either piece of jewelry ever again.

Even if Mark was cheating on me, I didn't find myself devastated at the thought, like I figured I should have been. Was it cheating if I was okay with it? Because I liked this. The solidity of Mark and the thrill of Shelly. I wanted to come home every night and have two people there to love me—or one there and one as a backup. I liked the idea of them loving each other, if only to solidify their love of me.

I LOVED MARK, I knew. The way someone loves a loud train that passes through their neighborhood at the same time every day. Familiarity. I only considered how I might have loved Shelly during the first time we were alone together. I had come home from work to the sight of her in the kitchen alone. She nodded and grinned my way.

The apartment was quiet and dark, only lit by the stove light. "Where's Mark?"

"Diane's house." Mark's mom. "He said he's staying the night there. His grandma is visiting." I didn't know that his grandma was visiting, but I took it as another sign of Mark's newfound thoughtfulness that he didn't let me know.

She walked out of the kitchen with two bowls in her hand. She was wearing Mark's clothes—a baggy T-shirt and his sweatpants rolled up on her hips, bunched at the bottom. "Do you want to shower first?"

"I have a lot of work to do," I said. "I think I'll do that first."

EXCHANGE

She stepped out in front of me, blocking my way. "Well, wait. You should eat first. You've been gone all day—you probably haven't had anything to eat, right?"

She only came up to my collarbone, but when she stood in front of me, I felt as if I could fit into the palm of her hand. She led me to the couch and ate while I cradled my bowl in my lap. Her spoon clinked and scraped in the quiet. I could feel her glancing my way, and the weight of her attention without the promise of someone else there to break it made my skin itch.

"Shelly, you don't have to stay here if you don't want to."

"Why would I be doing something I didn't want to do?"

I felt that I understood her better then, and I was in awe that Shelly was the type of girl who made decisions purely based on how she felt, as opposed to what she ought to do.

"You're closer to Mark."

"Mark is easy to be close to." She winced in the middle of her sentence, then suddenly puffed out her chest. "I think it's really amazing how you've been so cool about me hanging around you two. Most girls I know would want to claw my eyes out for looking in their boyfriend's direction."

I shrugged. She inched closer.

"You're not one of those worried girlfriends?"

"I can't really control what Mark does. Things like this are bound to happen eventually."

She looked taken aback. "Things like this?"

"Growing apart. Being left behind."

The scrape of her spoon stopped. "I can leave."

My hand shot out to grasp her arm, and we both silently watched where I anchored myself to her. The bowl in my lap tipped, and some of the soup splashed against my ankles. I watched it sink into the carpet. When I spoke, my words ground together in the back of my throat like broken glass.

"Shelly, it isn't that complicated to be near Mark. You can have him, honestly."

"What about you?"

"You want me?"

She scoffed. "I've been trying to get to know you this entire time."

I lifted my head up. I must have looked terrible, because Shelly's face softened into a look of pity as she reached out for my other hand.

"Okay," I said. My face felt hot as the hollow above my lip began to sweat. "Ask me some questions."

"What's your favorite place to eat?"

"I don't like eating out."

"What's your family like?"

"Broke."

"Why did you take a break from school?"

I let my head rest against the back of the couch. Shelly followed me, still holding onto my hand. The heat stretched across my face, a pressure that grew until my skin split, the sweat rolling down the fissure.

I told her how I was supposed to graduate the year before last. I wasn't used to struggling in high school. I did well because I had no other option. I stretched my body thin to cover everything I had to do—jobs, classes, internships. It didn't feel like there was any lead-up of exhaustion up to the day that my body began to change form. I would wake up a ghost drifting above myself, then slip into liquid, scraping myself off the ground to try and make it out the door as something solid. I would walk across campus, my body shifting with each step—a snarling dog, a beam of light, a pack of wolves, a rosebush.

My desk in class stood scorched, sopping wet—the ground littered in fur, dirt, teeth. I'd wait in humiliation for someone to say something, but no one ever did. They just scooted their desks away from mine to see the board better—looking past the brushfire, the flood, the blackbird. I realized I would have rather been reprimanded for what was happening to me than to have the people around me pretend to ignore my body—overrun with its own movement.

Mark did what he could. The shifting was most likely to stop when I was at home, and he would stroke my back while I sank against his body. I didn't know what would set me off next, and my mind flickered through all the possible reasons why I couldn't stay one thing, until all the small parts of daily life seemed impossible to carry. I didn't eat, I didn't go to class or work. The only action I could guarantee myself was the thin anxious sleep I slipped in and out of throughout the day—curled up within myself, a snake in my own decaying skin.

The worst part was watching. Watching the time slip away each time I blinked my eyes. Watching Mark try to maintain order around me. Watching the kids from my school pass my window—talking about clubs and course loads—and realizing I couldn't keep up anymore.

Shelly's mouth was drawn tight. "So you decided to take a break."

"I had no choice," I said. "I could barely move. It got

better, the more I rested. I could do the little things again, for the most part. I'm doing fine now in school, but I still remember how it felt to burn in public and have no one notice."

I closed my eyes against the heat.

"I'm just waiting to trip and get run over," I said.

My grip on Shelly had withered, but she only held onto me tighter, her nails leaving marks in my arms. She pulled me toward her as she leaned back against the arm of the couch.

Her hands reached around my body, stroking my back, clasped around the back of my neck while she pressed her mouth to my forehead. I heard her sniffle and cry, her tears dampening my hair limp with salt.

There's always been a dull humming in my skin—since my body ruptured—a threat, a rolling heat. A reminder my body was not mine to steer. For a moment I thought I felt it begin to peak, and I held my breath until I noticed this surge came from beneath her skin. I pressed my ear against her chest, and the thrumming there scoured my itching skin, until it seemed to finally be still for a moment—the movement beneath our skin met and roiled in time together, blurring what was mine and what was hers, so I could pretend it was just Shelly Shelly Shelly.

"Do you do stuff like this with my boyfriend?"

"We do other stuff sometimes," she said, "but not this."

SHELLY TOLD ME she wanted to steal a big-screen television from the Target she worked at. I couldn't make out the scale from the photo, so Mark and Shelly took a ruler and tape to make an outline on the wall in front of our couch, where it nearly stretched to all four corners of the room.

It was as if they were giving a presentation. They looked at me expectantly.

"Why a television?"

"Because we need one," said Shelly, and my heart ached. We. I wanted to shut up there, just so Shelly could keep telling me what we needed.

"It just doesn't seem like the type of thing you could steal quietly."

"I have a friend," she said. "He drives a storage truck. Trucks come by the back of the store all the time, and it won't be difficult to slide a TV out back, trust me."

"You'd lose your job," I said.

"I wanted to quit anyway."

"Quitting is different from being fired."

"Babe," said Mark, "what's the issue? You never had a problem with this stuff before."

"We've never taken anything that couldn't fit into our pockets."

"And maybe that should change," said Shelly. Her blond hair seemed limp and muddy. Dark circles lined underneath her eyes. "You of all people would know, once it's gone, it won't matter. You don't even have to do anything but wait for us to bring it back. I want this for you. I think you deserve this."

Mark and Shelly stared at me, waiting for my answer. I wanted to say yes for them. I wanted us to drive in a stranger's truck and take anything I wanted from a world trying its best to forget me—chew the road into rubble with big wheels, toss a trail of gum wrappers out the window. Shelly would drive, and I'd hold her hand while sitting in Mark's lap in the passenger seat, and the street would stretch out endlessly for the three of us.

I did my best to detach that image from the bright color of my dreams. I tried to render this picture of us into something that fit with the dull shades of the world I drifted through, but the image stood out as sharp and glaring as a knife.

"I just don't feel justified in doing something like that," I said.

Shelly bit her lip, as if trying to keep herself from crying. Then she drew herself up as tall as she could—her mouth bitter, her eyes stern. "But you're justified in stealing all your ugly little eight-dollar crop tops and lipsticks. It just adds up, doesn't it?"

She turned to leave, not toward the front door, but toward the room I shared with Mark. I watched her back as she stood in the hall for a moment, hovering at the bedroom door. For the first time since I met her, she didn't look bright. The shadows in the throat of the hallway swallowed her up—a small ghost in my apartment—before she opened the door and left us.

WE STILL SPENT time alone together after that. She would still show up unannounced, so that the nights I was home alone were spent sitting on the couch, staring at the empty space taped on the wall, waiting for a knock at the door.

I still noticed the smell of her on Mark—her shampoo and department store cleaner. I'd tuck my face in his chest and hold him close, close my eyes and pretend. I think he knew what I was doing. I had been held by him before, but he had never been held by me. He had never had me cling to him and stroke his hair. One night I tried to run my stilted hands across his back. At one point, I thought he had fallen asleep, until I looked down and saw that his eyes were open—wide and distant.

I moved out a couple of months after Shelly got mad at me about the television. I didn't say anything. They saw me packing my bags and clearing out my things and let me go. I left the necklace.

I saw them twice after that. The first time they were sitting at a cafe Mark and I used to go to. Before, I'd go there early in the morning to do homework, and he'd arrive a few hours later in sweats, just to steal sips from my coffee. Now they were there in the window. Shelly with her blond hair cut short around her neck.

I saw them for the second time on the news. A month after graduating I got my own apartment forty-five minutes away from where I used to live with Mark and Shelly. I had no furniture yet—just a recliner I had found at Goodwill, stuck with the footrest up. I sat with my laptop and saw a recent news story: a video of a chase between two police cars and a plain white delivery truck. The police pulled a new big-screen television out of the back while dragging two people out of the front. A crowd filmed the scene on their phones from the sidewalk. Mark had his face down, his brown roots showing, his lip curled in. Shelly looked up, spotted a camera, and grinned. She couldn't wave because of the handcuffs, but she bucked her arms like she wanted to. Her hair was short, dyed dark, and the necklace I'd left swung from her throat.

"Hi, Mom!" she shouted. "Hi, Caitlin! Hi, Emmy! Hi, Diane! *Oh*—hi, Quinn!"

I replayed that part in the dark of my apartment until my laptop died. Somewhere out there, my name lingered on a girl's mind, and my jewelry hung around her neck. I felt the shifting beneath my skin, the low, thrumming pulse. I imagined Shelly doing the same—sitting somewhere and remembering me not as something gone but as an ache that still anchored itself in her body—a familiar rhythm.

Pollen

FOUR ROWS DOWN in the locker room, I can hear that Trina touched a guy's penis while they sat in a slow Chick-fil-A drive-through. She speaks at a normal volume, but the metal lockers and high ceiling make her voice echo, which makes the squealing laughter of her friends in her row even louder. I can only catch pieces of what she says. *He rolled the windows up*—squeal! *I had to hold it at a weird angle*—squeal! *And there was this smell to it*—squeal!

Her words vibrate through my locker—or maybe it's just my own hands thrumming. I'm pissed at the girls, not because I'm just *that* excited to hear about the specifics of whatever the no-name high school guy's dick smells like, but because I want to know how Trina would describe something like the smell of another person. The only way I can think to describe a smell would be to say what the thing was. Grass smells like grass. My week-old gym shirt reeks like a week-old gym shirt. But does something like a guy's penis have a specific smell? Do all boys smell the same? If that was the case, what would keep Trina, who has several older brothers, from thinking that the high school boy just smells like her brother?

Hanna tugs on my sleeve, rolls her eyes, laughs at Trina and her penis talk, so I know to laugh back and follow her and the rest of my friends out of the locker room.

Everyone's swaddled in jackets and sweaters because somehow it's legal to force kids to run a mile even when the sides of the track are caked with mud from the rain, and everyone's breath clouds in front of their mouths, each puff gathering together in the air and making one big breath cloud to loom over us.

My friends talk and shuffle along the track, mimicking Trina's stretched-out beachy vocal fry, and laughing when they hear her talk ahead of us. I wait until my fingers turn numb. Goosebumps pop up along my bare arms, my ears and nose blush red, and—finally!—my teeth start chattering. Every time I laugh or speak, I sound like a stuttering television or dice clattering across a table. Hanna notices, she always notices, and she rolls her eyes at me. "Honestly, do you even own a jacket?"

She unzips her jacket, mid-trot, and hands it to me. "You're lucky I'm so tall that I can store more heat than you inside my body."

"I don't think that's how heat works," I say. I am lucky that she's so tall though. When I put on her jacket, it fits me like a dress, brushing up against the top of my knees and my arms like bees against flowers. Whenever I take it off, there are little pieces of green fluff from the inside that stay stuck to the hairs on my arms, and I can spend all biology class counting and lining them up on the table. I trot behind Hanna so that I can watch her ponytail swish back and forth like an old-timey grandfather clock. It's bright and blond among all the gray and black and blue gym uniforms, and I'm hazy neon green.

The mile passes quickly. I don't even feel tired. I barely notice how my group passes Trina's. I barely notice whatever it is Hanna mumbles to Trina as she passes. I barely notice how Trina's footsteps stop against the pavement.

The mile is over, and we're panting near the water fountain. I wipe the sweat on my upper lip with the front of Hanna's sweater. That smell is there again. I hold the jacket there. I can't put it into words, and for a moment I'm desperate for what Trina had to say, how she described the scent of another person. Maybe all boys smell the same, but certainly all girls don't. If that were the case, I would be fine with the smell of myself, but the smell of myself doesn't make my chest tight. Maybe it is the combination of myself and the jacket, Hanna's jacket, and the idea of the two of us being one unnamable smell together. Maybe Trina and her high school boy hotboxed themselves on some new smell in the Chick-fil-A drive-through.

"Ew. Are you smelling her jacket?"

I freeze. Trina and her friends appear in front of me and the jacket I still have pulled over my nose. The water fountain stops running.

I say no, which is a mistake. Trina already has her answer, and my voice putters out weakly.

I feel Hanna's eyes bore into the back of my head like worms in the wet ground.

Trina doesn't have anything very clever to say back. "Oh, well, it looked like it." Then she's off with her friends, laughing and squealing, glancing to look back at me like I'm a secret. My face burns.

Immediately my friends are rolling their eyes, brushing it off as something a stupid penis-and-sex-obsessed girl like Trina would say. Brushing it off like flower pollen, but the weight is heavy on me. I feel like I might sink. I want to.

Hanna and I hang back a little. She uses her height as a way to not look me in the eyes, and I don't know if her cheeks are red from running or not.

"I was just wiping away sweat, sorry if that's gross."

I wish it were true. I wish I could just be something simple and gross, like a penis-obsessed girl, or sweat on a lip, or sticky pollen flying onto arm hairs. Then I could be something she could see and grab and look at in the face and call gross. But I'm something else entirely now.

She says it's fine, but when we go to line up for badminton, she doesn't look at me, or choose me as a partner, or lean up against me while waiting for our turn like she does with our other friends.

I miss birdies and try to sort through the explanations swimming in my head about how I could lie to Hanna and tell her Trina mistook what she saw through the fog, and even if what she saw were true we're best friends, so what does it matter if I was sniffing her jacket, and why would she think I'm gross or weird or whatever she's afraid I am when Trina spent this whole period talking in specific detail about how she touched and smelled (smelled it long enough to put it into words) a boy's penis?

Hanna doesn't ask for the jacket back.

She Is Waiting

AVA STARTED FLOATING after the man took her from the park. They never caught him, so she didn't know what he looked like, but she remembered his hands—large knuckles shifting beneath pale skin. When he slipped her food through the wooden slats, his fingernails were rounded and spotless. The reflection of the sun turned his hands into light. Ava had wanted to stand tall on her tiptoes, not to escape, but to put his fingers in her mouth and shuck the light from bone.

As a child, Ava associated clean hands with competence. Her mother didn't use utensils when she cooked. She mashed ground beef in a bowl with the base of her palm, checked the temperature of boiling water with her knuckles, and turned over frying vegetables with her fingertips. When Ava saw that the man's hands were always clean, she thought, *Oh, he must be good at this.*

He kept her for a week. She had been tasked with chaperoning her little sister at the park, and she took that job very seriously, watching her pump her legs to thrust herself higher as she called out for Ava to watch her attempts at jumping to land on her feet. Ava remembered her sister had launched herself into the air, and as she watched her, her own feet came unstuck from the ground.

The man bagged her head and bound her hands with fishing wire. Ava did not hear him speak or even breathe;

it was as if she was alone in the sputtering vehicle as it shook on an unsteady road. When the car stopped, he gently guided her out by the hands and led her forward. She remembered the wind that day, snatching her breath. His grip loosened as they walked, until she was holding onto his fingertips, the way babies latch onto their parents as they're led to their first steps.

Suddenly the wires around her wrists snapped, but as soon as she began to lift her hands the ground fell out beneath her like a magic trick, and she fell.

She yanked the bag from her head. She was in a hole in the ground, staring up as the white hands laid down planks of wood at the opening, blotting out the circle of light. He came back every day just before the sky went dark, his hands sliding the planks back to drop her a plastic sleeve of cookies and a water bottle, which she devoured after a full day of the summer sun curing her throat dry. The heat wasn't as bad as the night, when spiders crept up her arms and she heard coyotes howl above her. The animals and bugs weren't as bad as having nowhere to piss or shit but right beneath her. And none of that was as bad as the tight space, sitting with her limbs folded against her body.

She remembered when they found her in the crest of a hill just five miles from the park. The firefighters had hoisted her up and out of the ground and held her up to a gathering crowd, who cheered as she stared down at all their faces—smudges of roaring light.

As they led her body through the hospital, the shower, into her mother's arms, who fed and kissed her and cried—*I'm sorry, I'm so sorry*—Ava kept her arms close to the numb tendril of her body. It was only when she was back in her own bed for the first time that she unwound her limbs as she stared at the ceiling, slowly stretching her arms out to her sides until her joints popped. Then, she finally let herself cry.

She wailed through the night even as her mother tried to console her and her little sister stared from the door, her fractured ankle bound in a plastic boot. Ava thrashed away from her mother's grip, splayed out on the floor with her arms and legs winging, hiccupping and leaking snot. She didn't want to be held, she didn't want to be touched. She wanted to vanish into something untouchable.

THE FOLLOWING MORNING, she started floating. Ava woke up in the air, the bedsheet draping her body like a tablecloth, haunting her own bed. Her mother put a stone in her backpack to keep her on the ground, but she could still feel how easily her limbs moved, how quick they were to rise up and tremble in the wind.

Her first few months back, Ava's neighbors left her gifts at her doorstep. At the grocery store they handed her free bags of kumquats and ripe avocados, the freshest meat in the deli. At the mall they gave her boxes of shiny boots and Mary Janes, dresses in her size saved at the front counter, fat rolls of hair ribbon and complimentary buttered pretzels. At school she received birthday invitations from boys and girls who weren't in her class, and if she went, they served her the first slice of cake. *Did you see his face?* they would ask. *What did he do?*

The neighborhood organized a fundraiser for her, which they promoted in the local newspaper by stating they were helping a struggling mother of two. Ava's mother did not want all those white people to think she was struggling. But she was struggling. So she used the money to pay for two sets of hospital bills, and to buy off her house, and to pay for a trip to Disneyland where Ava couldn't stop looking at people's hands, flinching every time someone reached in her direction. At home, she drifted higher, and her mother weighed her pockets down with more rocks, sewed sandbags into the linings of her coats, which Ava had to sit and sweat in while the heat ballooned her head dizzy.

Eventually the gifts and parties petered off. Adults stopped asking if she was okay and excusing her late homework, and her classmates only whispered about what happened to her when they thought she couldn't hear. She wished she had a different story to tell them. Something as biting as what they whispered about. The truth felt so incomplete to her, and when she recounted what happened to herself—the park, the hole in the ground, the hands— she felt her mouth hang open at the end, air hissing out of her mouth like a popped tire. She ran her hands over her body, gripped her bedsheets. After all that—*How am I even here?* She felt her pulse stretch the skin of her neck in crowds and she kept her eyes on windows when she was alone, riddled with the sense of waiting.

WHEN AVA LEFT for college, she moored herself with ankle weights hidden under baggy clothes, heavy industrial boots, and a backpack filled with rocks. She trudged across campus, glossed in sweat. She preferred the night classes, when she could get them, so that she could roll up her sleeves and unzip her jacket on walks back to her dorm, letting the night air carry the chill of the ocean onto her skin. At night, Ava could sink into dark corners and dim paths and ease her anxiety with the thought that she was hidden, not spotlighted or coaxed into the belief that she was safer during the day. She was convinced that in the quiet, she would hear it coming, and she would finally be able to see the face of what wanted to hurt her.

She met Freda this way. Ava had been listening to her sister's voicemail greeting when she saw Freda being kicked out of a frat party, ushered out by three guys. They didn't seem to touch her, they held their arms out to lead her away like trying to scare away a bird. When they got her onto the sidewalk, they backed into the crowd beginning to circle Freda. Ava inched into the crowd to see Freda in a sparkly dress, teetering in heels, her black hair crowding her face as she slashed at the air with a pink pocketknife.

"You wanna fuck with me?" she screeched, while the boys were caught between laughing and flinching away from her hand.

As the crowd edged back to dodge the blade, Ava was stuck watching Freda's back. She was waiting for Freda's confidence to flicker, for her to bend under the force of her own stupid choices. But she kept her eyes on the boys who carried her out. Ava was watching her so carefully that she didn't move out of the way of Freda's backswing, and she only noticed that she had been cut when the people around her gasped. Freda turned then, watching Ava touch the blood spilling from her cheek.

"You have to move," she said, breathless. Ava nodded, dumb and silent like a scolded child. Then Freda turned back to the boys, snorted and spit at their feet, and stalked off alone, the knife glinting in her hand.

Ava worked up the nerve to ask around about the girl at the party who had grazed her face and got a different story each time.

Freda Hsu was a lesbian witch who sacrificed one boy in a beach bonfire every month with a coven of ugly dykes. Freda was a prime suspect for arson in a string of wildfire cases in Santa Barbara. Freda kept men's finger bones in the pockets of her jeans. She sliced them off of guys she'd caught sleeping in the main library, and if you walked close enough to her, you could hear the bones rattle together as they shifted inside her clothes.

Freda was the one who found Ava the next week to apologize. She offered her a meal at a twenty-four-hour Denny's, and over eggs and French toast she told Ava that the reason she was waving a knife in the air at a frat party was because she caught one of the boys trying to put something in her drink. She said this casually, bent over her plate with a mouthful of food.

"And I'm not just going to be quiet about that," she said. She had yelled at the boy, making sure everyone heard her. Then as she was already walking away, that's when they tried to push her out the door. "I'm not just going to let some white boy put his hands on me and not have him regret it—you know?"

Ava nodded like she did know.

"But," she continued, "I would have never tried to hurt anyone who wasn't trying to hurt me." She gestured to the thin scar on Ava's cheek. "That would have never happened if I was sober."

Ava told Freda it was dangerous to threaten them. "What if they had called your bluff," she said. "If they didn't think you would do anything with the knife?"

"I would have killed them," she said breezily, and Ava held a gasp in her throat, her mind flashing through the stories of fire and bone.

Freda glanced up from her fork. "That's a joke."

"Yeah," said Ava, embarrassed. "Of course."

"But you've probably heard otherwise, right?"

The murmur of the diner swelled.

"I'm sorry," said Ava.

Freda laughed. "Don't apologize! I think it's kind of funny. I tell one person one thing, and now everyone knows something else."

Freda told Ava the original story—something she told a girl she had slept with as a freshman. Freda's older brother used to veer onto the sidewalks at night to crush animals under the wheels of his hand-me-down sedan. When he got into fights, he punched below the belt, bit off ears, and jammed his thumbs into boys' eyes. But he was only five feet tall, so he usually lost. When he did, he came home to win against Freda. He would kick her in the back of the knees, or yank her to the ground by her hair, or punch holes in the walls near her head. She was used to staring up at him from the floor, his body blotting out the light. During one fight, he had sat on top of her, pinning her body underneath his, with his arm against her neck. As black spots burned into her vision, she curled her mouth around two of his fingers and bit through the bone. He got off of her then, but in return he punched her in the mouth and knocked out a tooth. "So I still made a profit," she said to Ava.

She smiled and showed Ava the hole in her gums, leaning forward and pulling the side of her mouth back with her finger. She whistled high and sharp through the empty space. As she exposed the inside of her mouth, Ava wanted to flash her loss too. She told Freda about the hole she was placed in and the levitation that followed. As Freda watched her, Ava thought about the frat boys and Freda's unflinching stare. *Now she'll ask about what happened*, thought Ava, *or she'll act like I didn't say anything at all.* Her face burned as she worried about if she shared too much, if Freda would gawk at her.

Their fingers were clasped around their cups, their knuckles so close that Ava could feel the heat from Freda's body.

They ordered refills on coffee past midnight, until they lifted their heads up and realized that they were some of the last few people there, along with a pack of high school theater kids slathered in stage makeup and glitter, and a man blinking solemnly into a steaming cup.

They paid and left, and as they walked through the barren parking lot, Ava did not look at Freda's face, but she felt Freda's eyes on her. She struggled to swallow as she thought about the frat boys and the knife. The cut on her cheek felt tight on her skin.

"Can I see?" Freda asked.

Ava snapped her head up to look at Freda. No one had ever wanted to see her floating. They only wanted to speculate about the reason for it behind her back. Her mother had desperately helped her try to hide it. No one had ever asked to just watch.

Slowly, while keeping her eyes on Freda, she capsized her pockets, letting the stones and weights fall in oily puddles, and slowly her feet drifted off the ground.

Freda watched as Ava hovered above her. She reached

toward Ava, palms flashing in the glow of the diner sign. Ava braced herself, ready to be hurt, or cut, ready to have something taken from her. But when Freda grabbed her hand, she gently pulled Ava to her feet, holding on as she picked up the weights, dried them off on her pants, and placed them back in her pockets. Freda didn't let go when Ava landed; instead she linked their arms together, pressing their shoulders close as they walked back to the dorms.

Ava had never leaned against someone else to anchor her air-infested body. She only knew how to shrink under an outstretched hand. The air in her bones roiled like a wind tunnel, and her skin itched with the anxiety of waiting. She did not want to wait anymore, she wanted the snap of an end—to be able to look at the face of what wanted to hurt her and take back what it took from her.

Ava kept hanging out with Freda because she hoped that Freda's sharp edges would catch danger and bring it to her. Instead, Freda mostly repelled the danger—she was too quick to flash her teeth and bite back, a dangerous thing herself.

Freda worked as a resident assistant during their senior year of college. She only applied because she heard that resident assistants got a dorm room all for themselves, and she was determined to do the minimum amount of work it took to meet the needs of thirty freshmen girls on the seventh floor of the Santa Rosa Residence Hall. She expected the worst from remembering what she had been like as a freshman, but most of the girls were soft with nerves, being away from home for the first time. Ava came to the conclusion that the girls recognized Freda's sharpness, her willingness to bare her teeth, and might have also been tamed by the same rumors she had first heard about Freda before they became close.

Freda was their strict mother, and they attached themselves to her like a fish on a shark's belly, burrowing into her soft side. Whenever Ava visited the dorms and spent the night though she wasn't supposed to, Freda talked for hours about the girls: the homes they came from, how they were doing in class, the new friends they were making, as if they were small children and not technically adults. Ava thought that her own interest in the girls was just her being polite, until she found herself thinking about them outside of Santa Rosa Residence Hall, on her walks to class, thinking of what had happened to the girls since Freda last told her about them.

In turn, the girls came to know Ava as the girl Freda smuggled into her dorm room every other night. She had been worried they'd resent her and demand that she leave since they were watched more closely and weren't allowed to harbor bodies in their rooms after ten. But because they were soft girls, they treated her presence as a thrilling treat—they were in on something not allowed, and they liked to knock on Freda's door just to say hello.

Freda was Ava's only friend. Ava didn't know how to speak to others without thinking too much about how she looked, if she was saying the right words, where other people's hands moved. Freda was the first person who saw Ava's shifting eyes and long, distracted silences and waited patiently for Ava to come back from wherever her head went and continue speaking as if nothing had happened.

Ava didn't expect the girls to give her the same benefit

of the doubt. They got closer to her in increments, offering her a flat iron to borrow or a swig from their drink. *We were talking*, the girls said after a month of knowing her, *and we were wondering if you wanted to join us for a potluck on the balcony*. And Ava would wonder why any of the girls were thinking about her in the first place. She asked Freda why the girls were talking about her and being so nice to her.

"I just don't know what they want from me."

Freda looked up from the mirror where she was smudging black makeup onto her eyes.

"They probably just want to be your friend."

Ava did not know what to do with this. She sat among the girls, desperately keeping her shoulder flush to Freda's side, as the night air chilled everyone closer together. She watched them with a soupy awareness of the conversation, instead fixating on their teeth, the directions their eyes moved, the things their hands reached for. When they spoke directly to her, it was as if they did so through a glass panel, and instead of hearing them Ava made out the movement of their mouths and followed along with a script in her head to keep track of what she was supposed to say back, all the while feeling her body trying to linger out of her seat.

She left Freda and her girls and found that she couldn't remember anything that actually happened at the party. Instead, she ruminated over what she had said and did—if she had made the right decisions.

Some nights, Freda convinced Ava to sleep over.

Ava asked what the point was in Freda getting her own bedroom, and Freda told Ava that she could borrow her clothes if she needed. Freda was twice Ava's size and could see clear over the top of her head, so when Ava wore her shirts, they draped around her body in a way that made her feel small. They'd lie in bed together, and to keep Ava from gathering onto the ceiling like steam, Freda would drape her body over Ava's, rooting their legs together in the single-size bed.

The moonlight pooled around their skin through the window, and when she and Freda lingered awake, Freda pointed out the origins of scars she caught Ava's eyes on. A swatch of marbled skin on her thigh from where her brother threw a pot of boiling water onto her. A smattering of dark dots on her fingers from when she started picking at her skin in the fourth grade. A thin pink gash arcing beneath her knee from when she fell from the balcony while trying to sneak back into her house.

Ava looked at her own body in comparison. She rarely left the house as a kid, and her arms and legs glowed pale and flawless like the face of a new dime. She had spent a long time after the hole doing her best to not get hurt, and the evidence of all her work was there on her skin. She had never gotten so much as a bee sting. The longer Ava stared at her skin, the longer her breath stayed curdled in an inhale. Freda could feel the air ballooning in her chest.

"What's wrong?"

Ava tried to figure out how to tell Freda that she couldn't believe that she was still alive, and that she would have felt foolish to bask too long in the miracle of still being, after experiencing something that a girl shouldn't have survived. A Black girl even less so. Every day she racked her head over where that man was. If he was sitting in his living room watching television, his rough, chalky hands gnarled around a beer. If he was digging another hole into the ground. If he was looking for her.

"Nothing," said Ava, peering into the corners of the room while Freda rubbed her back. In the next moment, the room was bright with sunlight, and she was turning into the warmth of Freda's neck. Before she could blink the sleep out of her eyes she burrowed her nose deeper into the warmth, curled her body around Freda's scent, nearly lulled back to sleep before the air swelled. The heat was suddenly unbearable, and her skin itched while she squirmed free from underneath Freda's body.

Ava went home ruddied with a two-sided shame—that she couldn't let herself rest on Freda's shoulder and that she had let herself be lulled there in the first place.

TOWARD THE END of September, Freda called and asked Ava to come with her to rescue Chelsea, one of the Santa Rosa Residence Hall girls, from a party.

Ava's hands sweat around the phone. "Rescue?"

"All the girls last heard from her, like, thirty minutes ago. She'll be fine."

Freda met Ava at her door, already fiddling with the switchblade in her pocket. Ava tightened the straps on her heavy backpack.

The pathways around the campus at night were shadowy, only occasionally warmed by dim yellow streetlights spread too far apart. Ava peered down a path across from them where the tall classroom buildings stood half hidden in the dark.

Their footsteps echoed back to them until they approached a grungy late-night cafe tucked at the end of a steep hill. The building almost looked like a long black shed. Low ceilings, mismatched furniture, and novelty mugs. A space at the front of the building was sectioned off for a meek-looking band to mutter over the noise of the cafe, which was stuffed with preening groups of loud fine arts majors and brooding kids cloaked in black.

Ava stuck to Freda's side, feeling useless. She didn't remember which of the girls she had met was Chelsea, so she kept staring in the faces of strangers for too long. Their features and the music and the noise of the kitchen blurred together. She couldn't make out who she was looking at or what they were saying. She tripped forward and snatched up Freda's jacket in her fist, her stomach flipping as she struggled to keep her feet on the ground.

The two of them trudged down a narrow black corridor passing by the kitchen. The air turned heavy and sharp with the smell of urine. Through her squinting eyes, Ava could see that they were approaching a growing square of light. They came out the other end of the hallway onto a large cement patio circled by heavy potted plants with brittle yellow leaves gathering in sheets on top of the dirt.

Ava tentatively leaned back against the side of the building. A group gathered underneath one of the eucalyptus trees that towered through the center of campus and shrouded the cafe out of sight from most angles. The boys in the group were taking turns lobbing stones into the trees. The rocks ripped through the air like bullets. Each time, they flayed curls of skin from the tree and sent them scattering to the ground along with leaves and sticky seed pods. Several girls orbited around the boys, looking up at the tree and grimacing. Some were crossing their arms and pulling away past Ava and Freda, while another was whining desperately, asking one of the boys if they could all go home.

Ava didn't recognize any of these people. "None of these girls are Chelsea, right? We should go see if we missed her up front." Sweat rolled down her back.

Freda opened her mouth to speak just as the boys hit a bird with a rock. They gasped in awe as the black bird plummeted from the tree, floundering in a ball of its own wings, soaring low and fast toward Freda and Ava.

Freda ducked her face into the top of Ava's head and curled around her. Ava flinched herself into something still, her vision blacked out by Freda's chest. When Freda unfurled herself away from Ava, she kept her hands on Ava's arms.

"Are you alright?"

Ava's limbs thrummed. The points where Freda had her hands on Ava's body were hot. She could feel her thoughts starting up again—quick and ready to scold her for freezing, for not moving fast enough, for not being prepared—when she saw the bird. It writhed, its twisted wings flapping like an arrhythmic heartbeat, brushing up a cloak of dust around its body as it lurched up and slammed into the ground. The crowd of boys rushed over and watched, gagging and tittering.

Ava's feet disconnected from the ground. The tip of her boots pirouetted above the concrete. She grabbed onto Freda's arm. She was ready to tell Freda that she had to go home when a boy emerged from the dark hallway inside the building. He stood so close to her that his arm grazed her shoulder. He had a thin, serious mouth and a fluff of messy hair on his head. He stared blankly at the bird on the ground, then shifted his eyes to Ava. She turned her gaze away and saw the boy move out of her periphery. When he returned, he had a large stone in his hands. The air seemed to chill as he heaved the rock over his head and threw it down onto the bird.

Ava heard the commotion around her. The girls shrieking, another person throwing up in the corner. A name bounced around the crowd. *Lucas, that is so gross. Lucas just killed a fucking bird.* She felt the bodies shuffle past her, some to leave and others coming out onto the patio from inside to see why people were screaming. She felt Freda abruptly let go of her arm to speak with someone. But she couldn't stop staring at the bird.

Its wing peeked out from the rock, its legs like two little mangled twigs. It had been so frantic a moment ago, beating its body into the ground, and now she watched the cloud of dirt settle into a thin trickle of blood oozing from underneath the rock. She felt pulled into the silence that now consumed the bird whole, so much so that it felt like something she could fall into if she stepped in it.

The boy's shoes peeked into her vision. She noticed her own feet were back on the ground as well. The dim orange lights on the patio cut shadows into his gaunt face. His features were sharp but all contorted on his face—his mouth too thin, his nose skewing left, his big dark eyes too close together. The thing that stood out the most were his hands, too big for his body, like the paws of a puppy.

He looked between her and the bird, shuffling in place nervously. "It was going to die. I put it out of its misery."

He was still looking at her, as if he was looking for some kind of validation. Ava looked at the bird and nodded.

A girl with bleached ends and an apron came out and grimaced. She pointed at Lucas.

"You have to clean this up," she said.

Ava noticed that Freda had not gone very far. She had been behind her the whole time, speaking to a girl that she recognized from the party on the balcony.

"Chelsea's phone died," Freda said bitterly. Chelsea was still new to the campus and did not know how to get back to the dorms without it, so she followed Freda out into the hall to leave.

Ava watched Freda's back for a moment, until Freda turned back and called to her. She hurried to catch up, but not before glancing back at Lucas mopping up the floor.

She looked away too quickly to tell, but she thought she saw him wave goodbye.

AVA SPENT THE next week going back to that cafe, sitting on the patio and looking at the smudge on the concrete where Lucas had killed the bird. She'd go in the daytime when it was still light out and reluctantly leave at night, her floating feet slowing her walk home, as if she was trying to escape in a dream.

A small part of her came to the realization that she was waiting for Lucas, but it was difficult for her to understand why. Ava had never been outside her childhood home for long enough for anyone to grow close to her, and she spent too long staring at her own shoes to notice anyone else. She didn't feel anything when she thought about how Lucas looked and knew, if anything, that Lucas may have been sort of ugly. The kind of boy Freda would have turned her nose up at. Ava had turned down invitations from Freda and said she was busy studying, when in reality she had been skipping classes. She didn't want Freda to know where she was because then she'd have to explain why she was going there in the first place.

On the night that Ava saw Lucas again, she sat on the patio as the sun was just starting to go down. She found a spot on the outer edges of the cement circle, clicking at her phone and picking at her fingers to keep herself busy. The few people outside with her laughed and smoked together over the soft, scuzzy sounds of a guitar from inside. He stepped outside, alone and slouching.

Ava's pulse picked up in her throat as he eyed the people outside, group by group, as if searching for something, until he saw Ava. When they locked eyes he shot up straight and stood still like an animal caught in the woods. Panic shot through her for a moment, she felt the air surge beneath her. She wanted to leave. Then she felt stupid. This was why she was here, wasn't it?

She steeled herself, held onto the chair to keep herself down, and watched Lucas. He didn't walk directly toward her but lingered at the entrance and turned back for a moment, meandered slowly around the edge of the patio until he finally stood in front of her.

His arms dangled heavily at his sides. Ava gripped the edge of her seat tighter as she peered into his face. In the warm pink sunlight, he did not look any prettier than he had a week ago. A prickly patch of blond hair stubbled along his chin, and deep circles trenched beneath his eyes. His skin was so pale, it reminded her of curdled milk.

He brought his big hands together. Ava knew this boy was not the man who took her off her feet and put her in a hole in the ground, but as she watched Lucas's hands wring together she felt cold. Her skin itched as if infested with bugs. The light seemed to blot out around the edges of her vision, until she could only see the boy in front of her, the only source of blurring light, as if she was looking at him through a pinhole. Air raged through her body like a wind tunnel.

"Hey," he said, startling Ava out of her own head. His voice was quiet and raspy, as if he hadn't spoken in days. "My name is Lucas."

"I know," said Ava.

"You do?"

"I heard it," she said, "a week ago."

A silence passed between them, filled with laughter from somewhere else across the patio. Ava worried that she had said something wrong, but she didn't dare take her eyes off of Lucas. When he turned his eyes to the ground, she felt like she had won something. She exhaled and felt more grounded in her seat. She sat up straighter.

"Well," he said at last, "what's your name?"

When she told him, he repeated it.

"Ava," he said. "That sounds nice."

He glanced at the free chair at the table and sat down abruptly, scooting further from Ava, toward her and back again.

"Why are you sitting here?"

Lucas shot out of his seat. The chair screeched and fell hard onto the concrete. He picked it up and looked around sheepishly. "Sorry. I thought, well, I thought—we could talk."

"What about?"

He blinked at her.

"I don't know," he admitted.

"Why do you want to talk to me?"

He stalled.

"Because I like you?"

"You don't know me."

"That's why I want to keep talking to you. To get to know you."

For a moment, a sick feeling twisted in her stomach. She had an urge to be closer to Lucas, for a reason that still felt muddied to her, but this felt too close. The initial thought of Lucas's haunted eyes staring at her from across a restaurant table or kissing her cheek with his small, chapped lips made her recoil in disgust. Then she looked back down at his hands and remembered how he had hauled the rock above his head. She imagined Lucas grabbing at her, clamping his fingers closed until she bruised and sprouted bone. She imagined his hands would stay clean the whole time.

But maybe, she thought to herself, *since I've seen these hands before, I'll see it coming this time.*

She looked him in the face. "Lucas, do you wanna hang out some time?"

LUCAS INVITED AVA to his apartment for their first date. She wore wrist and ankle weights beneath her clothes and didn't let anyone know where she was. He told Ava his roommates were out for the day, so it would just be the two of them. They lived in an apartment just off campus, so the tenants were almost entirely students. Every other window displayed fairy lights, felt school banners, or cuss words spelled out in Post-it notes. Lucas's apartment was dark and muggy. A misshapen couch and a chair with a slash in the headrest sat in front of a small TV set on the carpet. The blinds were all closed, with one window taped over with duct tape. A mountain of dishes lurked in the kitchen, sitting in a gray tub of water. A collection of tied-off trash bags slumped together in the corner.

The blinds were drawn up in Lucas's room, and Ava squinted against the new light. His bed split the room, slender and pulled taut. It would have looked like no one had ever actually lived there, if it wasn't for the animals.

Big game sprung from wooden plaques along the top of the walls, their curling horns and antlers casting shadows onto the floor. A series of mice and rats crowded the shelves of a bookcase, posed in different scenes, their eyes shining black. A flock of birds hung from wires attached to the ceiling. Pigeons, swallows, fat white ducks—wings spread open in a still flight.

Lucas sat down on his bed with his hands clasped in his lap. Ava was still standing, staring up at the birds.

"Is this what you're planning on doing with that crow?"

His face was blank for a moment, before letting out a tiny "Oh." He twisted around to reach underneath his bed. He pulled out a folding food tray covered in newspaper. The body of the bird that he had killed had been cleaned off and gutted of its insides, leaving just the skin splayed open and flat. "It wasn't a crow," he said. "See? It's a blackbird." He lifted the side of the body and showed Ava a small patch of rust-colored feathers. "It's a red-winged blackbird. It will be prettier when it dries. I can show you when it's done."

"Thanks," said Ava. She couldn't find a place to sit other than his bed, so she crouched down near a shelf to look at a raccoon with a paper hat and a party horn.

"How do you find all these dead animals?"
"I used to go hunting a lot with my dad."
She paused and looked back at him.
"In California?"
"Yeah."
"That's legal?" she asked, feeling stupid.
Lucas nodded. "Yeah, sometimes I still go by myself."

He set down the tray with the dead bird and reached underneath his bed again. Underneath his bed was starting to feel like a bottomless pit, anything could have been pulled from it. Her brain raced with gory pictures of carrion and the crumbling floor of the woods. Instead, he pulled out a case—a slender black bag that looked like it could have carried a violin. He unzipped it and presented a shotgun. Ava had never seen a gun in real life before, so it seemed unreal in Lucas's arms—a spot cut out from a picture, a dark impression in his pale arms.

His hands hooked in place easily. It was the most relaxed Ava had seen him.

She stayed crouched on the floor, feeling the air swarm underneath her skin. She had not thought this through. She wanted to overcome him, survive him, and here she was, already stuck in a corner, alone and helpless under the thing that could hurt her.

He asked, "Do you want to try?"

She felt the sweat bead down her skin inside her jacket. "To shoot something?"

He shook it demonstratively. "It's not loaded." He beckoned her over, and Ava slowly rose to her feet to follow. Lucas placed the weight in her hands. It was heavier than she thought it would be. "You never want to aim at something you won't shoot," he said.

Lucas guided her with his hands—pointing the gun toward the ceiling, placing her finger on the trigger, aiming at a plain brown bird dangling from the ceiling. She couldn't tell if he was warm or if she was cold, but his touch burned across her skin. She imagined flames erupting around her neck, feeding off the excess air from her open mouth. A burning girl was just as bad as a floating one—both beacons for men who wanted to feel sturdier than ash or larger than a disappearing speck in the sky. She wanted to turn around and press the gun to the hollow of Lucas's throat, leave his hands useless and dirty with his own blood.

She pressed her finger down on the trigger. A dull click. The ring of silence in the empty apartment. The bird stayed floating in the air.

Lucas smiled at her sweetly. "What do you think?" She couldn't even muster up the strength to smile back. She felt like she had been cheated of something, even though she had been told what would happen. She handed the gun back to Lucas and sunk down onto his bed, lying on her back.

"It's cool," she said.

Lucas set the gun away in its case and sat on the bed next to Ava. He waited a moment before lying down next to her with his arms held stiffly to his sides.

"My dad would probably like you," he said.

"Because I can click the trigger on an unloaded gun?"

He laughed a little, mostly air, the drag of breath grating in his throat. "Yeah, actually. When he first had me try I couldn't do it."

Lucas told Ava about his father—a man who taught him how to swim by driving their boat out into the middle of a lake and throwing Lucas in to watch him flounder back to land. He first brought Lucas hunting with him and his friends because he thought Lucas was too soft—eight years old and afraid to speak in class, spending his free time drawing and building miniature huts from twigs and leaves and rubber bands. His father had shoved a gun into his hands, and he and several other grown men stood over Lucas and tasked him with shooting a duck in the water. When he missed, and the recoil of the shot shook his grip from the gun, the ducks in the lake scattered into the sky. Lucas's dad had scoffed, pushed him aside, and shot two ducks out of the air.

"Well," said Ava, "your aim has obviously gotten better."

"It's easier when I'm not being watched. I like knowing I can do what I want with my bag when I'm done."

Ava gestured to the bodies on the wall. "This?"

Lucas nodded. "My dad hates this. 'You're supposed to eat what you catch, not play with it,' he says."

Ava felt a little grossed out by the idea of shooting something and then eating it herself, but she figured that was more normal than killing something and letting it dangle from the ceiling.

Lucas could not keep a steady conversation going. Long silences stretched between them until he brought up another dead-end point about the types of birds he liked or the professors that he had that semester. The sun streaming through the windows warmed them both drowsy, and Lucas eventually nodded off in the middle of one of his long silences. She did not dare fall asleep. Instead, she watched Lucas and the spider-veined skin around his eyes as the air sat in her throat like a stone. She was waiting, still waiting for the bullet to fire out of the gun and tear them out of the silence. *Go ahead*, she thought as he slept, *make your move, put your hands on me. I'll make sure you regret it.*

OVER THE NEXT few weeks, Ava waited for Lucas to hurt her. When she stayed up at night looking out the window, she saw Lucas's face morph out of tree branches and passing car headlights, then disappear when she blinked. She dreamt of his disembodied hands reaching out to her in slow motion until she woke up sweaty and panting before they caught her. When she worked up the energy to walk to class, she drew her arms in close to her body, scanning the crowd for his lanky frame.

Once, Lucas caught her by surprise in public. He said her name inches behind her. She had flinched around and screamed, tripping back onto her ass. He apologized and reached his hands out to help her up, but she refused. He walked her to class and bought her a latte from a coffee cart while she privately seethed.

Stupid, she thought to herself. *Pay attention.*

Lucas sent her text messages: progress photos of the bird, videos he thought she might find funny, good morning and good night texts. Each time her phone pinged, her breath solidified in her throat. She realized she was anticipating some kind of sign. Something Lucas would say or do that would tell her now, now, someone is going to hurt you *now*. When she eventually read what he had sent and realized there was no sign, she would cry. She'd curl up in her bed and sob low and hard, until her eyes burned and her body ached from shaking.

Sometimes the texts were only from Freda, and Ava would cry then too.

She had hung out with Freda a couple of times during the day in the dorms with the rest of the girls. Ava was anxious about being alone with Freda because she knew Freda could tell something was wrong. She kept staring at her when she thought Ava wouldn't notice.

For their second date, Lucas made a picnic lunch and brought her to a green patch of grass on campus where students took naps and sunbathed. He bought her flowers. She couldn't focus on anything he was saying because she was too busy keeping one eye on his hands and the other looking out for Freda.

For their third date, Lucas suggested they go hunting.

"Since you have promise with the gun," he said.

The night before, she paced around her room as her palms sweat and her throat burned with rising bile. She didn't feel tired at all. Her feet thunked against the floor with her steel-toe boots and ankle weights. She couldn't get a full breath of air, as if it was all being siphoned to fizzle hot in her limbs.

She lunged for her phone when it beeped and scowled when she saw it was Freda. Her irritation left as soon as it came.

Freda was asking Ava to come over and spend the night. Ava looked out the window at the velvety sky. She did not want to leave now, not while she could feel Lucas's eyes all around her. Not while she could barely sit still. But guilt ate at her.

She gripped a pen in her hand and rushed over to Santa Rosa. She could see Freda at her window as she approached.

She kept her eyes on her as Ava walked all the way up to the front door, and Ava suddenly craved the warmth of her body. She had been so involved with Lucas, circling around his hand like a vulture. She had forgotten how good it felt to cling to someone she trusted. When Freda hugged her, Ava felt like she had taken her first full breath in days.

Freda closed her bedroom door behind them and immediately began bombarding Ava with what she had missed in the residence hall over the past couple of weeks. Ava listened while rooting through Freda's drawers for one of her T-shirts to change into. When she took off her jeans, Freda's voice stalled. Ava followed her eyes to the weights around her ankles.

She didn't say anything about them, she kept talking as if she hadn't seen them at all. Ava let Freda guide her to the bed like a half-deflated balloon and puzzle Ava's body against her side, pinning Ava's legs with hers.

Ava could have drifted off to sleep right there, lulled by Freda's voice rumbling in her chest.

"Ava," said Freda quietly, "are you mad at me?"

"No." A sense of dread fell over Ava.

"I feel like you've been ignoring me. I've hardly seen you lately."

Ava lay completely still in Freda's arms.

"I haven't been feeling well."

Freda adjusted so that they were face to face. She didn't pry, just waited in silence, lightly tapping at Ava's fingernails with her own.

Ava's words stumbled out slowly and clumsily from her mouth.

"I feel—stuck," she said. "I feel like everyone got over

what happened to me faster than me, but god—I don't know how much longer I need until I'm okay again, you know? Lately, I can't stop thinking about the hole in the ground. Sometimes it still feels like I'm there. Like I physically can't stretch my legs or put my arms out to my sides, like all that dirt is still around me. Whenever I look straight up I'll feel my eyes start to shrivel up and water. It's as if I never left."

She managed to avoid crying, but she was pressing one of her fingernails into the pad of her own thumb. She hadn't noticed until Freda pried her hand apart. A deep red divot emerged across the thin skin.

Ava wasn't sure how much time passed after she spoke. Her eyelids had started to feel heavy when Freda replied.

"Sometimes I have nightmares that I'm back in the house I grew up in. Except the halls are all, like, this maze. And I'm running and trying to escape because I can hear my brother yelling at me, or I can feel his hands brush against the back of my neck. It's like hell, and I just have to keep running until I wake up."

Ava listened in shock. Freda had never talked about what lingered with her when she left her childhood home.

"But then I wake up and I'm home. All my stuff is here, my body is here. Sometimes you're here. And that just makes everything that happens that day even better, because I'm in the aftermath of all that. No matter where I end up, it will never be there again."

"Don't the nightmares freak you out? Doesn't it—sometimes I feel like it's a warning," said Ava. "And if the same thing did happen to me again, it would be my fault."

Freda's eyes went wide.

"Something like that could never be your fault."

Freda ran her fingers along Ava's back. Ava could hear Freda's breath even out. She tried to match the rise and fall of her chest to Freda's. She wanted to believe her. She wanted to forget her hurt under the pressure of Freda's body. But she could still see and feel all the things that could hurt her while she was awake.

Ava did not sleep. When the sun leaked through the window, she slipped out of bed. Her feet were light on the ground, and she hurriedly put her shoes on before she could drift to the ceiling.

Freda's dark hair spilled along the pillow, her hands twitched in her sleep. Ava wondered if she was having a nightmare. She watched Freda, moving to help her before growing sick with the realization that there was nothing she could do but watch, useless.

She crept out the door, shutting it as silent as possible.

LUCAS DROVE A faded green car, its body peeling at the door handles. Inside, duct tape covered holes in the headliner, which was stained and pilling at the edges. The car hummed and creaked as he drove down a bare road. The gun rattled in its case in the back seat.

Ava's cell phone buzzed in her pocket. She had turned the ringer off before they left Lucas's apartment, and when she looked at it she could see two separate texts from Freda.

Checking to make sure youre okay
If youre not busy today we should hang out :)

Ava turned her phone off.

There was only one other car parked in the dirt-patch parking lot. It peeled away as they arrived, leaving them in a shifting cloud of dust, held alone in the bowl created by the black mountains around them.

Ava felt her legs shake. She thought they might have been aching from wearing the ankle weights so often. As they started on the trail, every step she took felt like it required the strength of her entire body.

Lucas guided her down a path shouldered by twigs and low branches that scratched against Ava's skin. There were steep drops in the path the further they went. Lucas offered to help her down, but she did it herself, crouching low to the ground first before stretching her trembling legs down the drop. Lucas held the gun in one hand, letting it rest easily against his shoulder, the barrel facing the sky. Ava's pen rattled in the pocket up her jacket.

The trees caved in on themselves, forming a black tunnel seeping with light. She smelled the lake before she saw it. It shimmered in the distance as a quivering silver line, then bloomed into view, the brown bodies of ducks lazing on the surface.

Instead of aiming his gun toward the pond, Lucas tilted his head up and watched an array of ducks lancing through the sky. He pointed it upward, clicked the trigger, and with a resounding pop, one duck in the group spiraled out of the sky, plummeting off into the distance.

His face was rosy when he turned back to Ava. "Here," he said, handing her the gun. He trotted off to go pick up the duck.

Ava stood alone in the brush, watching Lucas's back. Her hands felt strange while holding the gun, sweaty and slipping against its body as she tried to keep from accidentally triggering anything. It seemed to thrum with its own heat and energy, as if it would have moved and kicked on its own even without Ava's help.

Her mouth felt dry. She realized she was panting. Was it the hike here? Shouldn't her heart have settled by now? How does someone who is perfectly fine breathe?

"Pay attention."

She was startled by the sound of her own voice. The air whipped into a frenzy inside her body, raging inside her alongside the feeling that it was happening now. She didn't see what hurt her when it came the first time, but now she was looking at it. Not just disembodied hands, but a person who could be hurt just as much as she could.

It happened in one quick movement that felt beyond her control, as if someone was moving her arms with connected strings. There was no numbing click like the first time—the weight of the gun kicked back against her shoulder and clattered to the ground. The outline of Lucas's body spasmed to the ground.

There was only the flapping of wings and her unsteady breathing. She waited to feel the air expelled from her body, to feel her feet driving heavy into the ground as she walked, to feel like her limbs were connected to her, not hemmed to her joints by the atmosphere.

She waited until the heap shifted in the grass, and Lucas began to rise to his feet. In the distance, she could see his pale face flushed red, his chest heaving. He held his own arm, his hand hanging limp at his side, streams of blood ribboned down his skin.

He stayed completely still as he watched her, as if waiting for her to move first.

She felt her body drifting from the ground, untethered.

I have to move, she thought. *I have to move.* She turned and ran, slow and burdened by air, like running in a nightmare. Her feet lost contact with the ground. She kicked her legs but they only pushed her further into the air. The wind caught against her hollowed body, turning her loose into the sky, higher, until Lucas and his car shrunk down to specks blending in with the brush. She thought she heard him yelling, but his words were muffled by the air—his voice sounded like the whistle of air being released from a balloon.

Her phone slipped from her pocket and fell to the ground, but she was not looking down. She was focused on the mountains that had held her in the hunting grounds. Soon she would drift high enough that the bounds of the mountains would turn into a circle on the ground—a hole she could stare into.

She wanted to see it from that angle.

Nico and the Boys

EVERYONE IN TOWN calls Nico's father Baby, because he cries all the time. He cries when he's sad, of course, but also when he's angry or jealous.

After work at the repair shop, he comes back home to throw his leather jacket over his sweat-stained T-shirt and wet the front of his curly hair with water so that it sits limp against the edges of his brown round face. He clunks around in his beat-up truck, looking like a greasy clown in a noisy car, before stopping at one of two bars in town and sipping beer with women who mostly think he's cute in a pug sort of way, or funny, and that's it.

"Oh, Baby, you're so funny."

On a bad night, Baby gets into a fight with some guy tougher than him or just less drunk than him, and comes home before midnight with a new bruise or new cut, grumbling through cigarette smoke like a lonely train. On good nights, Baby comes home dressed in the damp blue morning and passes out on his bed fully clothed, the smell of perfume rolling off his body.

On either sort of night, Nico sits by the window, a baseball bat in her grip, waiting for the worm.

All the men in town call it a worm, the men who would talk about it. Baby isn't one of the men who talks about it, but he doesn't have to. Nico sees the evidence of its presence. She sees the shattered beer bottles and remains of food packaging strewn across the kitchen floor. She sees how Grandpa Jess's geraniums and coneflowers end up pulled from the ground and strewn across the backyard as soon as Jess gets them to sprout.

At night, the worm slips into Baby's head and leaves him silent and shaking, his sheets damp with tears and sweat, his eyes blown out wide, so that Nico has to call the repair shop and tell them that Baby isn't coming in today. On a bad night, the worm leaves Baby waking up screaming, waking up blind, smashing his fist into the furniture and racking his head against the wall until Jess leads him outside and tells him to sit there until he can calm down.

"You're keeping Nico up."

When Nico was little, Jess would take her back to her room and sing her old pop songs in his clumsy deep voice, until she faked being asleep long enough for him to leave. When he left, Nico would creep up to the window and stare down at her father's broad back, hunched over and black in the midst of cigarette smoke, the glowing red end of a skinny cigarette burning dimly in his shaking fist.

Now, at eighteen, Nico pours sugar around the edges of the house. She pours beer bottles out halfway and sets them outside the windowsills. She changes the lightbulbs in the house from the bright white bulbs to a dim, groggy orange. The idea is to get the worm to stay around long enough to partake in something else sweet, rather than just go straight for Baby's dreams. When she's pouring sugar around Jess's pale green sprouts, he laughs and says that sweet things won't stop the worm. Jess dealt with the worm in his own youth, and he says the only way to get rid of it is to talk about it.

NICO AND THE BOYS

"Like—talking shit?" asks Nico.

"That'd be better than what Baby is doing now, shutting his eyes tight, so he can act like it's not there."

Jess says that, as a man, it's humiliating to be brought to your knees by something you can't see. Something you can't even get your hands on because it's so slippery and small.

"That's why Baby gets in all those fights. At least when he gets his ass kicked, he can know that he got a few punches in."

Baby doesn't notice the sugar or the lights, but he notices the beer. When he asks Nico about the bottles, she panics and says that she drank them, brought them over to a friend's house for a party.

This catches Baby's attention, and instead of trudging over to grab his leather jacket, he sits down in the kitchen and tries to ask Nico about her life, tries to fit into the shoes of fatherhood. He trips over himself, not used to speaking to his daughter. He thinks that she is in middle school, when she's actually a senior in high school. He brings up a boy named Sonny Johnson who he remembers his daughter having a crush on, but Sonny Johnson moved out of town in the fifth grade. Finally, there's a break in the conversation where Nico awkwardly says that she won an award. Baby claps his hands together loud, and his watery eyes turn bright.

He tells her that's amazing.

"It's just for character, like how I act. It's not that important."

Baby tells her it's very important, he tells her she's got great character, and he tells her that he wants to be at the award ceremony. Nico's eyes water, and she and Baby look exactly the same. For the next week, Nico doesn't sleep. When she's at home, she's posted by the window, eyes dry from keeping watch. She lines her room with half-empty beer bottles so that the smell of booze seeps into her clothes and her skin and heightens her drowsiness. She keeps packets of sugar in her pocket and keeps her ear pressed to Baby's door when he's sleeping, listening for the sound of a slippery body slinking across the floor or onto Baby's pillow.

Every time Baby walks downstairs, Nico holds her breath. But Baby is better than Nico has ever seen him. His eyes are still watery, of course, but no tears fall. Maybe it's the sweetness rolling off her body, or the dim orange light warming the house, but when Baby gets home, he stays home. His leather jacket sits on the back of a kitchen chair, collecting grime, while Baby cleans up after himself. He throws away his cigarette butts. He only buys one case of beer for the week, sharing it between him and Jess. He helps Jess in the garden once, holding up a bag of mulch for his father in the sun while Jess leans over and pats down daisies. He cooks once, tries to make some mixture of beans and rice and sausage where the rice is soggy, the beans are tough, and the sausage is undercooked. Nico scarfs it all down and asks for seconds.

On the day of the ceremony, after school, Nico wears a green dress and scans the crowd for her father. He isn't there. With ten minutes till, she calls him, again and again and again. Each time the phone clicks to voicemail, her stomach becomes tighter, and her vision becomes blurred as she's filled with thoughts of Baby writhing on the ground and smashing his fist into the walls.

NICO AND THE BOYS

She leaves the ceremony before it starts, biking home in her dress on the dusty dirt road. When she gets to her house, she can hear the sound of Baby's muffled screaming, and she bursts through the door to see Baby standing upright, towering over Jess, his face red.

Everything is silent when she comes in, for a moment. Then Baby is on her.

His breathing is strained and his forehead is sweaty. He crashes his fist down onto the kitchen table, so that a piece of it crumbles away.

It must have been the lack of beer. Maybe he was finally sober enough to have a sense of what was around him, but he says he saw the bottles, on the windowsill, in her room. Saw the lights. Saw the sugar. He asks her what she needs all that for, taunting her, daring her to say that something is wrong with him. There's nothing wrong with him, and if Nico thinks so, she should toughen up and say it to his goddamn face.

Nico stares into Baby's crying eyes with a blank face. The only words she can get out are, "You missed my ceremony."

Baby makes an ugly noise in the back of his throat and grabs a beer from the kitchen. Jess pulls Nico away as Baby stomps out the front door, his footsteps echoing until he climbs into his chattering clown car and swerves off down the road.

The house is silent.

"I'm sorry, Nico," says Jess. He says that he told Nico the sugar wouldn't work, and that he would have gone to Nico's award ceremony, and that Baby just needed a little more time. "You get that, don't you?"

Nico nods and walks off to her room like a ghost. When Jess comes up later that night to tell her that dinner is ready, she opens the door just enough to tell him that she's not hungry.

At midnight, clattering metal and screeching tires pull into the driveway. A bad night. Cigarette smoke wafts into Nico's open window, and she waits until the sound of Baby's feet pounding up the stairs passes, waits until she hears his pained sigh of falling into bed. She wonders what new bruise or cut he has.

She gathers her suitcase and creeps down the stairs, out the door, into the moonlit blue night. The wind blows her hair around her closed mouth and kicks up dirt around her feet. As she walks away, the shift in the sound of the wind makes her turn her head back toward her house, small in the distance, completely engulfed by a coiling figure. A spectral white, tucking its smooth body into the window of her bedroom.

Nico drops her suitcase in the dirt, feeling her breath catch in her throat, her legs heavy and weightless all at once. She watches the worm creep into her home, the sound of its slick body scratching against the wood making her shiver. She keeps watching until it disappears completely into her house, so that white light shines through the windows and the wood panels, a flaming star stuck on the ground.

Then, she grabs her suitcase and runs away from the house and the worm, so she can try and miss the sound of her father screaming into the night.

Butterfruit

SHE CHASED THE slightest cool breeze in the air with her sweat-slicked nose, lifting her body up and ripping her legs away from the plastic-covered couch. Her mother pinched her knee and told her to stop fidgeting.

The relatives only spoke to Tess when they thought she was doing something wrong. But how could she do anything wrong when she was forced to sit perfectly still and sweat next to her mother until she evaporated into the air? It wouldn't have made a difference to the relatives if she *did* disappear. Every time she tried to speak, their cackling laughter ate up anything she had to say.

But they could hear Archie just fine. It was his eighty-ninth birthday. He held a crumpled tissue in his hand that he used to wipe his watery bug eyes every few seconds. He sat bundled up in a sweater and a cardigan, a crisp white shirt buttoned up to his hanging leathery neck, despite the fact that the flowers on the coffee table wilted in their vase and everyone else pulled at the collars of their shirts to let the damp heat escape their chests like a split baked potato.

The relatives threw their voices across the living room, but the moment Archie twitched his wrinkled lips to let out the high whimpering whine that was his voice, everyone went silent. Then they'd roar and laugh again like they understood him. Tess could not understand Archie when he spoke with his dog-whistle squeak, and she instead had to piece together the conversation based on the responses from the relatives.

They only seemed to talk about the beauty of the house. They pointed out pictures, cases of jewelry, silver spoons, the rings on Archie's hands, and asked him how much it all cost.

As Tess was forced to listen to their ogling in silence, teased by the soft trail of air that filtered through the room and disappeared before she could enjoy it, she found the house uglier and uglier. It was all low stucco ceilings, pale yellow wallpaper, thinning and cracked book spines, dust-coated edges of brown-stained portraits of dull-eyed dead people. Rusty ancient things like a letter opener or a magnifying glass that looked like a snow globe cut in half.

Her mother's favorite item in Archie's house was a case of crystal elephants behind a glass door. Different shapes and sizes, frozen in the midst of lifting their trunks into the air. Tess thought that they looked cloudy and tacky. They were pointless.

Archie, for all his feebleness, held a power over the room. When new relatives arrived, they all lined up to give Archie an awkward kiss or hug, with an awed hesitancy beforehand that made Tess think of peasants lining up to a king. They spoke to Archie cheerily, but the moment someone had to get close to his physical body, they grew small and stilted. In his chair, he seemed safer to be around.

When Tess had first arrived, Archie had still been getting dressed. She had walked toward a faded yellow recliner, but before she had even turned to sit, a relative had grasped her shoulder and said severely, "Don't sit in Archie's chair." At Tess's look of horror, they had all hollered while her face burned. But as the relative turned away, Tess spotted the pitying look in her eye, as if the chair was a lesson they all had to learn somehow.

Her freedom came when all the relatives coaxed Archie away from his chair and guided him into the sitting room to open his presents. As they went away, packed together like a slow-moving marching band, Tess unstuck herself from the couch and ran toward the breeze, following it to a cracked door near the back of the house, close to the kitchen.

In Archie's backyard, the grass dampened her ankles as she breathed in the gust of air that kissed her forehead. Tall bushes of pink bottlebrush and blushing roses curled around the edges of the fence, where small garden figurines hid among the patches of clover. A thick, tall tree grew in the corner. Its sprawling branches and twisting vines reached over the edge of the fence, heavy with a round yellow fruit.

Tess's breath caught in her throat at the sight of the fruit. She walked forward, in a trance, and reached up to grab one. Rainwater rolled off the swollen round flesh. As she plucked it, the branch stretched down and snapped back up into the air. Tess squealed in delight as more fruits toppled down into the grass.

When Tess took a bite, a chill ran through her teeth, but the bite in her cheeks and sweet taste across her tongue muffled the discomfort as the juice ran down her arm.

She ran inside with the fruit in hand to find her mother, and she found all the relatives in the muggy sitting room. A dim yellow light in the corner lit up the way all the relatives hooped and hollered, surrounded by more ugly things, as Archie shuffled back and forth in what must have been a dance. The relatives moved around him, singing and swaying.

She held the fruit up to her mother. "What is this?"

Her mother did not look down. She jutted out her hip and knocked Tess into the body of another relative. She steadied herself. "Do you know what this is?" she asked him.

He hardly glanced down at her. "Oh, what is that—a lemon?" He put his hands on her shoulders and moved her away. Tess went to weave herself back into the fray of relatives, but the bodies and breath churned the stifling air, and a gust of heat pushed her back out of the room.

She scowled and felt the heat rise in her belly. She stomped back out into the backyard and stared hard at the fruit in her hand. It couldn't be lemon. A lemon bit your mouth and did nothing to apologize; a lemon was wild. A lemon didn't allow her teeth to sink into its rind. She crouched over the fruit until her forehead touched the part that she had bit into, the yellow flesh leaving a kiss on her skin. Then she held it in the air and yelled, "Butterfruit!"

A few birds jumped at her outburst and escaped to the trees, but no adults came and told her to stop yelling or moving, so she threw it in the air and yelled her new name for the fruit again, emboldened by her loneliness. Butterfruit, for how easily her teeth sank into it.

She gathered the fruit on the ground in a circle around her feet and ate the rest of the one in her hand, chucking the seed into the bushes. When the seed clinked off of the body of a garden gnome, she crawled over and seized three of the figures. A garden gnome, a squatting frog, and a leaning mariachi player. She set the three of them in front of her and forced them to watch her eat. She leaned back in the cool air and dug her free hand into the grass so that wet dirt caked up in her fingernails. Gray clouds rolled along in the sky, so that the sun could not reach her. She savored the sweetness of having a crowd witness her greediness, like a cruel king. She reveled in the joy of discovering her own beauty in this house, a bright and cool relief in a fading, muggy prison, that no one else wanted but her.

She ate until her stomach was round. She walked back into the house, a butterfruit in her hand. The heat hit her hard in the threshold of the back door. She wanted to gauge how close her mother was to leaving. As her mother was the second youngest person in the house, she was often left out of the conversations about how Archie used to whoop the older relatives as children.

But when Tess turned the corner into the sitting room, her mother looked like she fit right in, grinning with the other adults as they gathered around a large painting looming over a teal couch. They spoke loudly. Archie was gone.

"I'm getting this one," said a relative. She splayed her hand across the surface, thick globs of paint recreating a choppy sea. "No one else even look at it, because it's mine."

"If you're getting this one, then I want the picture of Auntie Judy."

"Wait, I wanted that too."

"There are probably more pictures of her around here somewhere."

Another relative grabbed one of the many bells that lined the top of the empty fireplace. "I want these."

Another relative called, "What the hell you want those for?"

"Might be worth something." He shook the bell hard, and the ringing matched up with the laughter of the relatives, bright and sharp. Her mother put her hand over her mouth delicately. She said, "I still can't get over those elephants."

"Well, I sure as hell don't want them."

Tess slipped beneath the crowd, unnoticed. The rest of the house stood silent and empty. The only sound was the relatives' laughter echoing through the halls, growing distorted and distant as she crept further away. In the living room, a fly clinked around the yellow overhanging light that lit up Archie's stale face. He sat like a life-sized doll left behind by a child, looking small in his own clothing. His mouth hung open and his bug eyes stared unmoving at the wall, while his arms draped over the armrests of his chair as if his sleeves were filled with straw.

A sick feeling rose slowly in Tess's stomach. She stood still, breathing heavy, until Archie sputtered and blinked. He wiped his eyes with his little handkerchief, then looked over to Tess. He smiled, all small yellow teeth pushed close together, black in between. Tess smiled softly and raised her hand to say hello, but Archie's eyes fell on the fruit in her grasp. He pointed with a shaky finger and said, in his shriveling voice, "Those trees still grow peaches."

Tess's face turned pale. She sprinted out of the living room, through the sitting room, elbowing the adults out of her way. She burst out the back door, feeling the water from the grass splash onto her bare legs. She fell to her knees. The fruit rolled out of her hand as she stuck her fingers down her throat. A crowd of relatives gathered at the front door, crowing with concern and confusion. Her mother rushed to her side, and Tess felt the scratch of her fingernails against her neck as she held back Tess's hair. The tears and snot dripped down into the grass, mixing with the golden pulp.

Be Good

I LEFT AFTER slicing off the top of my finger in my parents' barbecue restaurant. On the same day that I got my stitches pulled out, I shaved my head in the front seat of my car, bent over a plastic bag in the green light of a gas station. Some people shaved their heads for spiritual reasons. I cut off all my hair in a frantic search for relief. I had suffered from dandruff since I was thirteen, and I had hoped that going bald would finally relieve me of all the itching and flaking. Instead, it just revealed how bad my dandruff actually was: hard scaly patches, red sores from picked scabs, and raised spots that stretched down the back of my neck. The worst part was seeing the shape of my head, which, just from feeling it, I had always feared was uneven and now I could see how lumpy it looked, sloping lower on one side with a dent at the crown—a divot that gathered sweat and oil.

None of this helped with the scratching. Now that I could see the problem like a map on my head, it just made me want to cull the sores raw and scratch until the flaking stopped. Because I figured at some point it had to stop. At some point I could scratch away at my head until all the skin that made up my old self was gone, and I could be someone new, slick and unburdened.

I parked outside of a Starbucks and used their Wi-Fi to find out what to do next. I had nowhere to go, or nowhere I wanted to go. I had friends I could probably call, who would have been nice enough to let me stay over—but they were all living these new, shining lives I felt I wasn't allowed to touch. They had new jobs as nurses, teachers, artists. One of my old friends was even a mother now, with a husband and a house and everything. I watched her give birth, letting her anchor her nails into my hand while her giant baby fissured her body in half. She bled and shit herself, but when she finally got to hold the baby in her arms she couldn't stop staring and kissing his milky forehead. Then I watched her lick the top of his head—a tentative little taste. I couldn't help the way my stomach turned—part disgust, part jealousy. I was looking at two new people.

I didn't want to be a burden. Instead I looked for roommates online until I saw a Craigslist ad that read: 3 GOD FEARING WOMEN SEEKING PIOUS FEMALE TO WORK IN EXCHANGE FOR HOUSING.

I was running out of money and had no job, so this was the only apartment I could really afford. I stopped by Party City on my way to the address and bought a dark blunt-bob wig, just long enough to cover my neck.

The god-fearing women lived near the beach, close enough to see the ocean sprawled out behind them and close enough that the pedestrians used space in front of their house and around their neighborhood as a path to the sand, dusting the black concrete white. All houses by the beach looked different: gray cement blocks, glass walls, black spires, swinging rose windows. The women lived in a cottage that was pink-shingled and sun-faded, lined with white wood rails. Rows of pinwheels speared their front lawn, twitching weakly in the placid winter day.

BE GOOD

I had expected the women to be old, but when I knocked, they formed a wall at the door, looking more like a group of sorority girls out of a film—blond, bright, giddy among themselves.

The girl in the middle spoke, her voice laced with anticipation. "Are you Jane?"

It took me a moment to remember what I had called myself. I stood at the edge of all things Jane could have been, briefly overwhelmed with choice, before I remembered that Jane was an absolute nobody, and that was what I wanted for now. I said yes, and the girl smiled, her teeth as white as paper.

"I'm Brielle. Welcome to our home."

The women—Brielle, Morgan, and Violet—led me through the cottage, a dollhouse rendered in white. Their shoes clicked across pale waxed floors. I asked them if I had to take my shoes off, and they said, *What? No, of course not.* The sun beamed in through the windows and transformed all white surfaces to light. The couches, the rug, the countertops, all glowing in the reflection of the mirrors that seemed to adorn every wall, and a dainty chandelier that cast splinters of light through the kitchen and living room.

A single black tripod stood in the center of the living room. Their home was also their base for work—a YouTube channel where they analyzed the Bible in the context of what it meant to be a young woman loyal to God. I sat locked between their shoulders on the couch while they showed me some of their videos on a laptop. "The Role of Women in the Church." "How to Be Stylish in a God-Honoring Way." "Sex and Relationship Q+A: How to Maintain Your Purity." In one video, they filmed bits of a live show they performed a few months back, where a crowd teemed with white preteen girls all donning baby pink T-shirts bearing their channel title across the front, *God Has A Plan For You, Girl!*

They were planning to self-publish a book—part autobiography, part guidebook, part Bible study. They were too busy writing and running the channel to keep up with merchandise sales, another large part of their business. Their garage overflowed with boxes of plastic-wrapped shirts, coffee tumblers, keychains, purity rings—every other item bedazzled with pink and white rhinestones.

"And there's your bedroom," said Brielle, then caught herself, "*if* you decide to stay." The spare room probably used to be a closet, a thin metal bar hemmed around the walls above a single bed, a slender wooden desk, and a bedside nightstand. There was a thin strip of free floor space, about as wide and tall as my own body. The rest of the house carried the scent of the ocean, salt on the wind, but this room was heavy with the scent of household cleaner.

It was a scent that lived in my heart, and I could parse it out like a hound. Bleach-washed sheets, lemon-scented disinfectant, newly unpacked IKEA furniture: cardboard, plastic, new cold metal. The god-fearing women stood by the door, watching me, waiting for my answer. I imagined them mopping the floor and moving furniture into a closet they gutted of its clothes, and that's when I began to see them as my saviors, their pale, unscarred hands scouring a way for my new start.

I HAD WORKED retail jobs since I was thirteen, and most of them left me with some new fear or sense of disgust.

BE GOOD

I associated the smell of sizzling meat with scraping spit-logged gum off the bottom of tables in my parents' restaurant. I was a vegetarian until my freshman year of college. At sixteen, I worked at a grocery store, and the sight of people licking their fingers to open produce bags gave me a hand-washing habit that left the backs of my palms thin with rash. After a lice outbreak at the daycare center I worked at, I started washing my hair every day to try and scrub away the feeling that something was crawling on my skin.

I realized I was the type of person who could never have alcohol after buying a handful of mini bottles after my shift at BevMo! and chugging them all within an hour, gin torching the inside of my throat, singeing my nostrils, and lighting up my chest more than a fire ever could. It would have been better if I had thrown it up, because it might have taught me a lesson about gorging myself on things that only knew how to take, not give. Instead the heat settled into my limbs like it belonged there—a warmth that lit my eyes and made my blood slow like it actually wanted to stay in my body.

I stopped then, because I was worried I'd never be able to stop, but I found a replacement fire in a substance available at any job: cleaning products. Not to drink, but to inhale and let envelop me.

It was already something I sought out at work—taking opening shifts at the daycare so I could be greeted with freshly waxed floors, offering to scrub grease off the counters in the restaurant kitchen, feeling relief in the combination of Comet and Pine-Sol. My routine for peace of mind was standing in a quiet room and reversing the damage of everyone who had sullied it, creating a new day.

I even brought the tradition to my own bedroom at home with my parents, where I pressed new rubber gloves up my nose and sprayed my sheets until they were wet with Lysol. I drenched my windowsill in Fabuloso, wiped my fingerprints off every surface, and got dizzy off the scent of being washed away.

I tried to avoid touching anything in my new bedroom, to preserve the feeling that no one had ever lived there. I would shuffle across the short stretch of floor in slippers and touch the few pieces of furniture with plastic gloves. At night I would fold the duvet and sheets back and gingerly set myself on the bare mattress, willing myself to float, my body tense until I finally sank to sleep.

The god-fearing women cooked and ate breakfast together in the mornings. I'd wake up to clinking utensils and the whirring of a juicer, the smell of citrus and cooked meat. The first morning, I couldn't decide whether I would join them or stay back, until my hesitancy made the choice for me. I expected I'd have to put my own breakfast together in a stranger's kitchen, or just go out to eat, until I walked by the kitchen and saw a plate draped with a paper towel and a sticky note that had my name written on it in loopy middle school girl handwriting: *Jane*.

Fat strips of bacon, toasted bread, a pile of scrambled eggs, jam that came in jars topped with crimped gingham cloth. I ate alone at the kitchen table while they got ready to film in their living room. Brielle gave me a little wave, and Morgan stopped to ask if I liked the jam. Her mother made it herself and sent a few new jars to the house every few months. Brielle and Morgan wouldn't touch it, so it was typically up to Violet to finish off the jars before they could accumulate in their fridge. I told her it tasted great.

"Now Violet won't have to finish them off on her own," said Morgan. I glanced up at Violet to try and smile at her, seeing as how we were both apparently tasked with eating all the jam in the house. She had dainty features in a full face, white-blond hair poised in doll ringlets. She looked back at me with a still expression, giving me nothing, before turning back to her work.

I packed orders at the same kitchen table loaded with stacks of T-shirts and shimmering merchandise, printing shipping labels and creating structure from a random list, organizing by size, by state, by bedazzled Bible cases and plain pink Bible cases.

From where I worked, I could watch them film in the living room, sat on the couch opposite of the window, where the excess light against the white walls, the mirrors, the pale champagne hair around white faces flooded the lens. They had to wait for the picture to readjust when they got up to grab something or leaned forward too close to the camera—the screen blowing out detail and leaving a blur of light, a white-hot suggestion of a girl.

A small part of me hoped that I would listen in and become indoctrinated in their faith. I wanted to become just as devoted as the teenage girls who cried at their meet and greets, thanking the women for steering them down the path of God. When I couldn't, I took it as another sign that I was missing something vital, something others had that allowed them to be swayed and comforted by things like God.

Brielle answered an email from a thirteen-year-old asking if it was okay for her to wear makeup, writing that, according to the Bible, wearing too much makeup would demote them to prostitutes. She swept a hand beneath her face—as unmarred as still milk—and said, "I only wear tinted ChapStick and a tiny bit of concealer for days that I get a pimple."

Of the group, Morgan looked the most severe, sharp boned, her mouth a thin line. Her voice was low, a cleaver hefted down on a monotonous tone. She was also the most nervous in front of the camera and would pause in between shots to take deep breaths and read lines from a piece of paper that would always end up crumpled in her sweaty hands.

All their videos ended with a reminder that their book would be available for preorder soon. I initially expected this to be fake, or written by a person whose name would not end up on the front, but nearly every other night the women would stay up until it was so late it was early, hunched over laptops with splayed-open Bibles beside them and enough loose paper to act as a tablecloth. In my room, I'd fall asleep to the sound of the women reciting and debating the meaning of verses. I listened but didn't understand. Instead of hearing the stories as parables I could use to carve out a clean life, I affixed my desire to the stories about transformation: staff to serpent, water to wine, a woman to salt. It made me regret that I didn't have much to contribute when Brielle or Morgan tried to talk to me about scripture. I didn't have real faith in anything that didn't have the power to physically change what it touched, the way bleach made a room simmer with absence, the way the meat slicer at the restaurant bit enough of my finger so that it healed at a slant.

I worried that they would sense my lack of faith the same way my mother would sometimes make us get up and leave in public spaces, drop everything and go with little warning. *That guy*, she'd say, *did you see that? He gave me a bad feeling.* And the next day she would call up someone she knew from the diner or mall we abandoned just to prove a point. They'd say, yeah, actually, last night we had to kick a guy out for climbing the bar or harassing some girls, or shooting a gun at the ceiling. How did you know? My mother would look at me like *See? What'd I tell you? Don't I always know?* If the women could tell that I wasn't as godly as them, they didn't kick me out for it. Instead I felt like they showed me parts of themselves they didn't show their preteen devotees.

Brielle had an obsession with reality television and could name all past and present housewives of Beverly Hills like the names of saints. Kim, Dorit, Garcelle, Lisa Vanderpump, Erika Jayne. "Ooh," she crooned, "Erika. That icy bitch, I love her."

Morgan sewed her own modest clothes, but also kept a separate secret wardrobe she collected from thrift stores. "I would never wear them out," she said. "But they're fun to wear at home." Black corsets, red miniskirts, leather harnesses, chunky platform boots. She wanted me to try on some of her clothes, and she faced the other way while handing me a short black dress with puffy sleeves, the neckline cut knife sharp and deep. She stood behind me in the mirror and rested her hand on my hip. "It looks good on you. Keep it. To wear in private, of course."

Violet still wasn't speaking to me, and the other women's gradual attachment to me made her even more distant. She didn't look at me when I walked into the room; instead she looked up or just past me, her gaze grazing the side of my shoulder like a bullet. She kept her line of sight so steadily fixed away from me, I wondered if she actually saw something that stood just beside me. I pictured a glowing demiurge floating above me, dropping into these women's bone-pale living room to decide my fate by giving me a thumbs down.

She seemed holier to me than the others because I hadn't seen any lapse in her devotion. We shared a bedroom wall, the only two on the bottom floor. Sometimes if I stood close enough to that barrier, I could hear her voice muffled by the static of the ocean. I had initially assumed she was on the phone, since I couldn't hear anyone answer back, but the rhythm of it made no sense to me. It wasn't like a call or a prayer—she repeated broken lines of conversation, her voice dipping, stopping, sighing, before pitching up again, quickly moving to a new line to mutter to herself. Sometimes it would stop, abrupt and cold, and I couldn't hear anything after that but the click of her bedroom door.

There were no cuts in the videos she filmed, no chaff to sift through while she rifled through Bible verses. She was the closest to bringing me to godliness. She spoke with a clear, bright authority—her tongue as efficient as a silver fork. "Ultimately, God is a being of forgiveness. You can ask for His help and dedicate yourself to Him even if you've previously led a life of sin. We are all sinners, we must all pray for His forgiveness at some point."

WHEN SUMMER CHARGED through town, I realized that there was no air-conditioning in these apartments and homes by the beach. The ocean was supposed to carry in the cool air, but we could only feel that chill early in the morning before the sun came up, and even then the air was wreathed with the promise of heat.

The women left the windows open, letting the hot air gather up the curtains and the hems of their dresses, so it looked like they were always seconds away from being wafted into the sky. They would tie their hair up in blond ponytails knotted against themselves like the ropes of a ship, letting the air kiss their goose necks, letting the sun singe them pink.

I still wore my shiny Party City wig, a black shroud surrounding my neck, a trap for heat. I felt like I could only take it off in my room, where the warmth gathered and bloomed with no windows for it to escape through.

Brielle said I should keep my door open, especially at night, to let the cool air in. I told her I was fine, but I didn't tell her that I was afraid of them seeing me on the bed with my sheets pulled back, my hair growing out in patches, still raw and peeling against my shoulders like a decaying body.

The sweat made me wake up every morning with my face glowing, my thighs sticking together, and the smell of my body sharp. I couldn't bring myself to lay on my bed this way, fearing how I'd make the mattress damp and it would catch the scent of my armpits in the threads. Instead, I slept on the floor, letting the strip of cool air kiss the top of my head from beneath the door.

One night, while the heat kept my sleep thin, I woke up to Violet's voice coming from her room. It was different from her usual murmuring; her voice crept out in crooning bursts, almost like singing, so soft I could only really hear her by holding my breath. It stopped, and I almost went back to sleep before she spoke again. I couldn't make out words, only the hiss of air from her mouth, the click of the door, and footsteps. I expected to hear her walk toward the bathroom on the opposite side of the house, but instead the creaking sound of the floor grew louder and louder. A shadow blotted out the dim light creeping from underneath the door. I turned over, startled, and scrambled to my knees as the door cracked open.

A large silhouette stood in the doorway. A hand felt for the light switch on the wall, and we both peered at each other in the new blinding light. His hand scratched at his dark, bare stomach. He was naked, soft and slick, grogginess marring his face until his eyes focused on me—bald, wide-eyed on the floor.

He gasped and cursed, stumbling back and reaching to cover himself. His heel caught against the rug behind him and he fell backward, the corner of a side table clawing into his back as he fell.

He writhed against the ground, his moaning like an animal. Violet's door swung open. She rushed out in an oversized T-shirt, her hair slept-in and frothing around her shoulders. For a moment, the light of the moon blotted out the details of her face, making her skin glow like a new dime. Then, the shadows caught her face as she looked down at me—devastated.

She yanked the man up to his feet and pushed him out the front door as he protested.

"My clothes," he cried.

"*Stop talking*," Violet seethed. I stood and watched from my door as Violet ducked into her room and came out with a pile of clothes. She did not let the man get dressed as she shoved the clothes into his arms and pushed him out of the house, pressing her body against the door as she clicked the lock.

The heavy pulse in my throat mimicked Violet's haggard breathing. She glanced back at me, and I froze. *I am next*, I thought, *another shadow shucked from this house*. I fell back into my room and closed the door, huddled against it the same way Violet had been, as if the women were planning on breaking it down. I was suddenly hyperaware of my own body—my fingers sticking to the wall, the sweat pooling on my upper lip, my skin tugging at my scalp. I felt that I had to atone for these things. For being dirty, for being unprepared for a danger that had flitted so obviously in front of my face before it struck.

The women's voices met in the hall hushed and quick, then suddenly bubbled up in laughter. They wished each other goodnight, the hallway light flicked off, and Violet's bedroom door clicked shut. The night was quiet again.

MY PARENTS MOVED from a town of six thousand people in Texas to San Diego when I was little. They talked about it like they had moved from another country. They never meshed with the foam and sea salt of the ocean, they complained that they could smell it even while inland, and my father said that living near so much water made people flighty. That's why California bred all those potheads who spent thousands of dollars on rocks and metal bowls and oils, he said.

Being around too much water dislodged you from your good sense.

My mother was born from dirt. Her own mother had molded her with rough hands, so her body was firm but misshapen, bulging at some points, caved in at others. She could smell the air and tell when rain was coming, so she would know when it was time to wait out the rain inside or under the balcony, lest the water beat her skin to mud. Before leaving for California she spent weeks looking up earthquakes, typhoons, tsunamis, any disaster summoned by water. The ocean made her anxious because she wasn't sure if she would be able to smell a tsunami or an earthquake. I got caught in a rainstorm in our first year in San Diego and had to run home, my shoes squelching, my dress plastered to my body. My mom saw me at the front door and said, *You couldn't smell that? You couldn't tell what was coming?* I said no, and she looked at me and shook her head.

When I was still in grade school my mother would sit me on the floor between her knees and grease my scalp, braid my hair taut for the day. When she was done, she'd bring me to the mirror and wipe the extra product on my forehead away with her wrists, leaving them shining in the bathroom light.

You're a beautiful girl, she'd say, less like a compliment and more like a prophecy, willing it into existence.

I'd study my face in the mirror, look at my body from every angle with a handheld mirror in my bedroom, and not find a single flaw. Her word had deemed it so—the same way she summoned cold wind to nip at my bare limbs on walks to school after I argued with her that I didn't need a jacket. Or the same way she'd walk into a room, look me up and down, and tell me my period was coming, even though my body never gave me any warnings like bloating or cravings. Within hours of my mom saying so, I'd find myself soaked in sweat and unsteady with nausea, passing clots the size of my fist.

I worked in the barbecue restaurant they opened and owned themselves. As business owners, they often talked about what they owed. They owed rent, they owed paychecks, they owed their lives to the enterprise they committed themselves to.

I would tell them about things I learned in school, and they'd tell me how they never learned those things when they were kids. How lucky I was that they gave me this opportunity to educate myself on quadratic equations and W. E. B. Du Bois and Chaucer. In every meal I ate, every book I read, every day under the roof over my own head was a moment to be grateful that they unstuck themselves from the stability of poverty to give me a chance to see the flecks of gold moving in the sand under the ocean. The least I owed *them* was to keep up their hard work. When they talked about my future, the restaurant was always there, something they tied me to. No one asked me if working there was something I wanted to do. My mother just said, *When you graduate college, you can start taking on more responsibility in the restaurant.*

What if I decide to do something different?

What for? When we've given you all this? She had spread her hands out, gesturing to the crumbling parking lot, the peeling tables, the open grease trap. *We'll pass the restaurant to you. You'll work here, and one day your kids will work here.*

When the meat slicer took the tip of my finger I didn't panic or cry out for help. I watched the blood pulse down my hand and languished in the thought of letting it take my whole hand, my arm, my body. I wanted to summon my mother's ability of calling something into existence so I could say, *Actually I won't make it through this, my life is done here*. So I could have fallen into a heap on the ground instead of waking up to live a life someone had chosen for me.

I HAD EXPECTED the house to be empty the next morning. The women had been planning a shopping trip in order to film a video about the state of women's clothing—"Are Trendy Clothes Modest?" Brielle had not seemed optimistic. *Maybe we'll be surprised*, Morgan had said. *Maybe the immodest clothes won't be so bad*. Like she didn't know.

I assumed Violet would have gone with them, but she sat at the kitchen table waiting for me.

She sat up when she saw me. "Jane!" She sounded relieved to see me, as if she thought I wouldn't be there for some reason. Her grin strained against her face. "Hi, come sit down."

She gestured to the table where my breakfast, usually covered and set aside, was laid out on a plate: eggs, bacon, toast. Morgan's mom's jam and a glass of orange juice set on the table. I instantly wondered if she had spit in it. I sat down and looked for any evidence of tampered food, loogies, spit bubbles, suspiciously churned scrambled eggs. It looked fine. *It's probably fine*, I thought. The women had been cooking my breakfast the entire time I'd lived there, and there had been no problem before.

Maybe, I thought, *Violet has been spitting in my food this entire time.*

I pushed the eggs around my plate. Then gave up on that and spread jam on my toast. Violet watched me the entire time, hands clasped around her own drink, the glass sweaty and dripping in her palms. Her smile stayed on her face but didn't meet her eyes, which looked more distressed the more time passed.

Finally, she coughed into the silence. "So—last night was pretty crazy, huh?"

"I guess," I said. "Yes."

"I'm so sorry that you had to be bothered like that."

I shrugged. "It's really no problem."

"I mean, you live here too. You deserve your privacy just like any of us."

She spoke to me as if she were filming a video, direct, rehearsed. I nodded and smiled like one of her teenage devotees.

"And to be barged in on like that by that—man."

The word *man* struggled to leave her mouth, catching in the back of her throat. The way I had seen him, a stranger blending into the dark, he barely looked like a man. As the two of us were scurrying on the floor, it felt more like we were two identical animals. I couldn't help thinking how Violet might describe me to him—*that woman*—my humanity also stuck to the roof of her mouth. Would he feel sick when he heard it too?

"I'd understand if you would want to talk about your experience—get some answers."

I shrugged. "I think it's just a misunderstanding. I don't really need to know anything."

"Well, please do not misunderstand that I am strong in my faith. I do not waver in my loyalty to God. I am also sure in my belief that our God deals in forgiveness. If I ever stray, I assure you, I do my part to beg for the forgiveness which I know He is so willing to give."

"Um, okay."

"I am also loyal to my audience, because I know they look up to me and use me as a way to understand the Word of God. And I would hate for them to have a misunderstanding about me."

She watched me, searching my face for comprehension.

I gasped. "No," I said quickly, "of course not. I hope you don't think I was planning on trying to tell anyone anything."

Violet sighed, her small eyes soft in her round face. I had never seen her look so grateful, like someone who actually worshipped.

"That's so good to hear," she said. "I mean—it would probably be really hard to find new housing on such short notice."

"You were really thinking about moving out?"

She gawked at me. "Oh, no. Of course not. I would never. This is my house and my home."

My face fell. The ice in her glass clinked as it melted and shifted. "Were you going to kick me out?"

"No," she said. She set her hand on mine. "No, because there's no problem. I know you won't tell."

The implication hit me like a mallet.

I set my knife and toast down. The food had all gone cold and spongy by then.

"Well, it's a good thing you never had anything to worry about in the first place."

"Are you angry?" she asked.

"Of course I am. You were planning on kicking me out over nothing."

"Not over nothing—"

"Over me seeing your boyfriend?"

"He's not that," she said quickly.

I rolled my eyes. "Fine. Over me seeing whatever guy you had sex with last night."

She flinched. I worried that I was definitely going to be kicked out now, but instead of pointing me toward the door, she clasped her hands together in her lap. Not praying but thinking. "I'm a good person," she said quietly.

"Sure, whatever," I said. "I don't really care."

"Jane, you can't blame me. There are a lot of people who would love to catch me or any of the girls in a situation like this. Do you know how many blogs and forums and videos there are trying to accuse us of being sinners and hypocrites—and that's with no evidence. They would die to be in the position you're in. Excuse me for being cautious around someone I barely know."

"It's not my fault you've been ignoring me since I got here. At least the other girls talk to me. They actually trust me enough to not threaten to kick me out."

She huffed. "It's not as if you've been trying to get to know me."

"I smile and say hi and you ice me out. I'm not going to beg for you to look at me and say hi back. I don't watch your videos. I don't give a fuck about you."

The heat gathering under the wig crept up my face. Sweat pearled at the base of my neck.

I ran my hands under the kitchen sink and brought them to my neck, hoping the air could catch against the water and cool me down. Violet watched me from the table.

"Are you like—sick?"

"What?"

She nodded her head in consideration for a moment before flipping her curls with her hand.

My hands fell like weights. "No, of course not."

"Oh, sorry. I just assumed. Why then?"

I figured she was making fun of me. Even in the dark, she must have seen.

"I mean, shaving your head, that's like a thing some girls do now, right?" She turned her nose up. "I would never. But it's like a modern, cool girl thing, right?"

"It's only cool if it looks nice. The bald girl still has to be beautiful."

She shrugged. "So what's the issue?"

I hated the airiness in her voice. For the first conversation we had ever had with each other, it seemed like I didn't hold any weight in her mind. I was something she tried to push out of her house only to pull it back to see what was inside, tossed in any direction she wanted. She tilted her head like a curious bird, and I wanted her to be disgusted by whatever she found in me.

I didn't take the entire wig off, but I peeled the bottom of it up and craned my neck to the side so she could see, the scabs pulling and weeping blood as I did so. Violet stood and walked up to me. I flinched as she placed her hand on my back. "Is this it?"

"It's all over my head," I said.

"That's not that bad," she said. She walked in front of me. "Dandruff is easy to fix."

"Well, I haven't been able to."

"How often do you wash your hair?"

"Every day."

She looked startled. "Oh—you're not supposed to do that. Not with curly hair."

I could help letting out a small laugh. Violet, with her bouncy platinum coils, trying to tell me about how to take care of my hair. As if I didn't know. As if she didn't spend her childhood with brushed-out frizzy hair and smoking flat irons the way any white girl with curly hair did before she realized she couldn't actually wash her hair every day and had to put product in it. As if my own mother didn't have to shake me and say, *You are not white*, after she told me I should wash my hair every day because a girl at school told me I was disgusting for not doing so.

"I can help you take care of your hair," she said cheerfully. "Are you trying to grow it back out?"

I shrugged. "I just want the spots gone."

She only brightened more. "I could do that, easy."

"I'm not letting you touch my hair."

"I used to work in a hair salon. I worked on all kinds of hair—including my own." She fluffed up her hair for emphasis. "I can help you clear up your scalp. And in exchange, you don't have to tell anyone about last night."

"I wasn't going to tell anyway," I said, my voice clipped.

"Please, she continued. "Let me help." *Let me*, she said. But it didn't feel like I was letting anything happen. She held out her outstretched hands an offering that felt more like the impending talons of a bird. I could only stand and let her take me.

I WANTED VIOLET to balk at the task of trying to revive my hair. She stood behind me while I sat in her bedroom, and I waited for her to cringe and pull back. Instead, she began calling me into her room twice a week so she could scratch at my scalp with a skinny comb, sprinkling white flakes onto my shoulders. She doused my head in tea tree oil and apple cider vinegar, and the scent of them stung my nostrils and ballooned in my lungs. She watched me lean into the bathtub and wash the smell out of my hair with shampoo, guiding my head down so I could watch the soapy bubbles gather and pop down the drain.

I was still angry at Violet, less because she was ready to kick me out and more because she had pierced through this new person I was trying to be. My blank slate was now cracked with the same things that had weighed me down before. And wasn't I letting Violet revive even more of my old self by just sitting quietly and wishing for the will to be defiant? Letting her bring me to where she thought I should be. I imagined my mother watching me let a white girl mess with my head while I seethed in silence. *But you whine and complain when I do your hair*, she'd scoff.

Violet and I still didn't talk much during the day, but the silence felt less hostile now. When I walked into a room, she'd look at me, instead of pretending I wasn't there. I understood that she felt what I felt with the other girls. When someone brought up sex before marriage, it was the same as when the topic of skimpy clothes or reality television came up with Morgan and Brielle, when the air between the two of us sparked with the heat of a shared secret.

Morgan and Brielle assumed I would keep their secrets.

Violet was still anxious after a month into doing my hair. When she checked my hair for shedding, her voice doll sweet—"I just wanted to make sure we're still okay. Are you still upset? You still aren't going to tell, are you?"

I finally asked, "Is it really that big of a deal?"

She showed me the comments, the conspiracy videos, a blog called jesusfreaks.pizza dedicated to pausing their videos at unflattering frames and ridiculing them. *I knew a girl like this in high school, she killed herself. These are the types of girls who do anal and still call themselves virgins. Die slut. These bitches can burn in hell. Morgan is low-key stacked. She'd look hot if she didn't dress as a pilgrim. Whenever I see their faces on my feed I get the uncontrollable urge to run them over with a truck.*

And the forums of people trying to catch them in their hypocrisy. *So Morgan talks about dressing modestly but we can see her bra strap at 4:32. Interesting how Brielle says it's only okay to listen to music with a godly message, but here's a video of her in 2013 at her birthday party with "Starships" playing in the background. Cropped photos of Violet standing next to men at her church. So which one of these guys is sticking it in?*

She finished washing the conditioner out of my hair in the bathroom. While she toweled me dry, I asked, "So are you not allowed to have a boyfriend?"

"That guy you saw wasn't that," she said. "He couldn't be that." She was quiet for a moment. "Besides, either way, it's a sin—what I've done."

"I thought God dealt in forgiveness."

She narrowed her eyes at me. "He does."

"Don't you think if there's a God, He'd have better

things to do than worry about who you are having sex with?"

She yanked the towel away from my head. "If?"

"Yeah, *if*," I countered.

She rolled her eyes and faced me toward the wall. She uncapped something she had been rubbing into my scalp—something that smelled like menthol and made my head tingle. "If it's part of the guidance He gave us to live a holy life, then yes, He does care."

"What's that mean anyway," I asked. The bite of menthol hung sweetly in the air. "A holy life?"

"It means leading a life devoted to God. A life devoted to being a good person."

I made a grumbling noise as she rubbed at the base of my neck. Most of the sores on my head were gone. Even as she scoffed, her hands were steady and gentle.

"Don't tell me you're against being a good person too."

"Who are you being a good person for?" I was genuinely curious.

"Other than for God, I just want to be good. I want others to look at me and know I'm good—someone thoughtful, someone virtuous. Following God is a way to do that. Not only is my faith what lives in my heart, but it signals to others that I am dedicated to good. Everyone wants to be a good person, Jane."

Her voice lingered in the air after she spoke, the pulse of her words as resounding as the echo of a drum. Her breath on my neck made me shiver. "I don't think I do." A warmth settled over my body. It felt so nice to say. "Yeah, I don't want to be a good person at all."

Violet paused. "You're lying."

I laughed. "I think I just want to be happy."

"So you would be okay with being happy, even if you knew that the way you got your happiness was hurting others?"

I turned the thought in my head for a moment. A life where my limbs weren't bound with guilt. One where I didn't feel like I owed a debt for breathing. I imagined the joy of doing what I wanted, focusing on my heart and no one else's.

"Yeah."

I turned to see if this was the thing that would finally make her disgusted with me, make her loathe me as much as I did her. Her face was tight, as if she were in pain. "That must be nice," she said quietly. "I couldn't do that."

BY OCTOBER, my hair had grown back short and crisp. Enough to cover my head and rake a comb through it. Enough to retire my sad Party City wig. I had assumed Brielle and Morgan had known it was a wig, but when I came into the kitchen, Brielle smiled and said, "Oh my goodness. You got a haircut! So cute!"

It was cool enough outside again for me to lie in my bed instead of on the floor. The sheets still smelled new, bleached and untouched, but my pillow adopted a faint scent of menthol and jojoba oil that I couldn't wash out. When I looked in the mirror, I felt unrecognizable from the person who I was before I left, frantic and bald in the front seat of my car. It was a relief now to look at myself and feel nothing, when before my own skin felt like a suit I had been stitched into. So, when I saw a missing poster stapled to a telephone pole in Pacific Beach, I stared at the photo wondering where I had seen the girl before, until I realized I was looking at myself.

It was an older photo I took with my parents. Their shoulders boxed me into the cropped photo. My hair was long, frizzy, and pale at the ends with damage. I was smiling in the photo, but my eyes looked strained, stamped dark with fatigue.

I ripped the photo from the pole. My parents' phone number was on the poster, along with a name no one had called me in almost a year. They weren't even offering money, I noted. They had none to give away.

I couldn't find any more posters as I drove home, and the one I had found burned against my hip in my pocket. I kept waiting for the panic to set in. I thought it was possible that the women already knew. They all finally had a secret against me, all heavier than the little secrets I kept about them. They would call my mother, and she'd tell me I was coming home, and then I would because her word would latch itself into my chest and drag me toward the fate she had built for me.

But the panic never came. It loomed over me but never crashed. I knew, of course, that it was me on the poster, but she felt so far removed from myself that I couldn't imagine any consequences that happened to her would affect me. The girl in the photo was locked into a future she didn't ask for, but not me. How could I be? When I was on the other side of the county with hardly any hair and a different name.

I folded the poster and tucked it under my mattress at around the time I expected Violet to call me into her room, but she never did. When I got tired of waiting at my desk, I stood and knocked on her door myself.

She stood looking haunted in the doorframe. When she grabbed onto my arm and dragged me into her room, her grip felt like it could break bone. Her eyes were rimmed red, and her hair was pulled loose from its curls, frizzy and limp.

"What's wrong?"

Without looking at me, she turned to dig through the top drawer of dresser. Her nails scratched against the bottom, and she pulled out a white plastic stick. She showed it to me.

"I'm pregnant," she said in a small voice.

I hesitated. My first thought was that Violet would want this, a baby to raise under the same godly rules she followed. I pictured the social media opportunities. A baby Instagram account, *God Has A Plan For You, Girl!* infant onesies, all the monetized content for the next nine months alone: gender reveal, baby shower, mommy morning routine.

But none of those things would be possible if she was sitting in the frame by herself.

"Whose is it?" I asked.

"That guy you saw here a few months ago."

I nodded.

"Well?" she said, whispering.

I matched her tone instinctively. "What?"

"What do you think?" I couldn't tell what exactly she was asking me for.

"Violet, why does it matter what I think?"

"I need someone's opinion," she said.

"Don't you have a family or God or something?" I tried to keep my voice gentle, but Violet flinched anyway. "Can't they help you figure this out?"

Violet paced the floor for a moment, staring down at her shoes before sliding to the ground, her back up against her bed. "If I went to my family," she began, "my mom and dad—they would want to celebrate. They would be disappointed in me, of course. I've done something so irresponsible and wrong. I've sinned. But even after begging for forgiveness, I know they would celebrate a—life."

Her breath hitched on the word *life*.

She pressed on. "I don't want their opinion. And I don't want to figure this out," she said, her voice brittle. "I want someone to tell me what I want to hear right now."

"Do you know what you want to hear?" She nodded in silence. "Well, if you already know, why can't you tell yourself?"

"If it was just me, I think I would be able to convince myself out of it. I would talk myself in circles until it was too late. We are lost without guidance, but I'm especially lost. If someone else told me what to do, I'd be able to trust in that more than myself."

"Why me?"

"Because I know you, and I know what kind of answer you'd give me."

I thought of the photo tucked beneath my mattress. When Violet said she knew me, she meant this new version of myself.

I bent down to sit in front of her.

"Think about the way you live your life now," I said. "Do you like it? Because if you had a baby, everything would change. You'd basically be a new person." I had no experience with the fear of being a mother, but I knew all about being a child. "And you'd have a new person looking

BE GOOD

up to you, needing you to make decisions for them all the time. And who's to say it would even be worth it? Because they might not even grow to like you. I would think about yourself. You already know what everyone else would say to you. Only think about yourself. Do you want to feel like a different person?"

VIOLET ASKED ME to come with her to the clinic. I was allowed in the waiting room, but she would have to have the abortion alone.

A few other people were there. A woman with a stroller, another doing crossword puzzles on her phone, another young-looking girl whose eyes welled up every few minutes. A few men took up the waiting room chairs as well, all of them tense and silent—a few with wedding rings on, and one scrawny teenage boy.

Violet slouched in her chair and stared at the ceiling. She wasn't in her usual white; instead she sat swallowed in a black hoodie and jeans, her hair pulled back from her face and tucked into her shirt. She looked like she was in disguise. She probably felt like she had to be. I wondered if anyone in the room would have recognized her. If any of the younger women had watched her videos. Maybe they were a part of the hate forums, maybe Violet's voice needled around in their thoughts, stitching them in shame.

Her own videos were haunting her too. She kept her eyes on the ceiling as she leaned over to whisper in my ear. "I can never make videos about modesty ever again."

"Now you can talk about new things if you want."

She gave me a sidelong look. "I'll just have Morgan and

Brielle talk about the modesty topics. Which leaves me with what—roles in the church?"

Her hands were tight around the arms of her chair. I couldn't think of what I could say to console her. I had assumed I would be nervous here too, that all the nervous energy from the patients would rub off on me, but the waiting room smelled like antiseptic and clean plastic. The smell of it soothed me in a way that I was sure it never would Violet. *Take a big whiff*, I wanted to say. *This is the smell of a burden being lifted from your shoulders.*

Finally I said, "I like that forgiveness stuff you talk about."

A nurse called Violet's name before she could answer back. It was as if I was one of the men left behind in the waiting room, except there were no stakes for me here. I wasn't losing a potential child or gaining any relief from having a potential child taken off my hands. I had tried to convince Violet to tell Morgan and Brielle, since I thought they were close enough friends that, even if they didn't want her to go through with it, they would be appropriately emotional for her in a situation that required more softness than what I knew how to offer. Violet didn't think so.

"Even if they did agree with what I was doing," she had said, "which they wouldn't, I wouldn't want them there. Seeing me like that."

I think I understood. For Violet, and the other women, it wouldn't have mattered if they had support from each other. The biggest issue would have been being seen as the thing they tried so hard not to be, being seen as what they claimed to be their opposite.

I expected to wait a while, but before I could even question if Violet was going to go through with it, she was already done, walking back into the waiting room with a little baggie of pills.

"Are you feeling okay?" I asked on the ride back.

"The lady in there was so nice to me," she said, looking far off and distracted.

"Well, she isn't supposed to bully you," I said softly.

The cramps started the next day, and she was stuck lying in her bed all afternoon, her skin clammy and white like a flayed fish. We told Brielle and Morgan it was period cramps. I kept checking on her to answer her weak request for water or Advil, to turn her heating pad on when it clicked off on its own because it had gotten too hot. She only got up to use the bathroom, drifting from her room in a white nightgown like a ghost.

When Brielle and Morgan went upstairs for the night, Violet knocked on my door. She swayed on her feet, her face tight and eyes unfocused.

"I can't be in there alone right now," she said.

"Do you want me to come sit with you?"

"No." She looked around my room. "I want to lie down in here. Can I?"

I almost said no, on instinct. But she looked so heavy, slouched over, cheeks puffed up, swaying as if her insides were filled with a storm. Any moment her skin would split, and she'd collapse and become ocean runoff. I glanced back at my bed, made up and untouched. I stood aside.

Violet stood at the edge of my bed for a moment, before lifting her gown up above her head and letting it pool onto the floor. A red splotch from where the heating pad had scorched her skin stood out on her pale belly. I expected her underwear to be white, stark bleach pure, but she wore a gray sports bra and a pair of faded striped panties that were loose at the hem.

I held my breath as she crawled into my bed, tucked herself beneath the sheets, and pulled the duvet beneath her chin, blond hair splayed across my pillow. It felt like a miracle that I wasn't sick. I didn't want to question it. Instead, I tried to creep back into my desk chair. Violet sat up.

"No," she said. "Come here." She pulled the covers back and pat the spot next to her, close to the wall.

An itch churned beneath my skin. *But I'm different now*, I thought. *I have a new name and no hair and no hang-ups about my own body. I owe nothing and have nothing to give.* This is what I told myself as I lay down next to Violet, my frame stiff as she leaned into me, the tips of her fingers resting against my arm.

We didn't say anything to each other for a while, just let the distant clamor of the ocean seep in through the walls. Violet's breathing periodically hitched, a labored, whining exhale as her body folded into itself, then slack relief in her face when the pain ebbed back.

In this quiet space, she said, "I know it will sound stupid to you, but I still kind of feel like a mother."

"How?"

"I feel different. I wanted things to stay the same, but I still feel different."

A slight sense of dread grew in my stomach. "I hope I didn't convince you to do something you regret."

"No," she said. "This is what I wanted. I knew that." She

began tracing patterns on my arm with her nail. "I think one day, though, I'd like a girl."

"A daughter," I said.

"Yeah." There was a smile in her voice. "What about you?"

"Ugh. None. Children are just a disappointment."

"There's no way you really believe that."

"Eighteen plus years of trying to make them into what you want, and then they just seem to end up doing the opposite of what you want." I turned to her. "Like, when you have a daughter, she'll definitely be some kind of hedonistic lesbian devil worshiper."

Violet laughed. "I'd still have no choice but to love her and be proud of her. It would be impossible not to—she'd be mine."

She looked at me with such softness in her eyes, I had to turn away. I wouldn't have been able to look at her the same way she looked at me.

"I bet your mother is proud of you," she said. "You're a beautiful girl."

"No," I said. "I don't think I am." I meant it, and the words felt true. Instead of arguing, Violet rolled her eyes and curled into a steady sleep, her breath even. "I'm not beautiful," I said again, with no one to hear me. "And no one is proud of me."

I SLEPT IN a way I hadn't experienced in a year—deep and heavy, lines from the folds of the sheets pressing into my skin. I sat up in my grogginess, and it took me a while to see that the door was open, leaking moonlight into my bedroom.

Violet's space on the bed was empty, and in her place, a dark spot stained the sheets. I ran my hand over it and felt that it was still wet.

I got up to check if she was okay, expecting to find her in the bathroom. Instead, the bathroom was open and empty, the light left on. Violet sat on the living room couch, framed in her white gown. She held a piece of crumpled paper in her hand, but I didn't realize what it was exactly until I saw that girl in the photo.

Violet looked up at me, then back at the photo. She held it up, comparing my face to what she saw on the poster.

She shrugged. "I think this girl is beautiful too."

"No," I said quietly. "I don't think so."

"It was crinkling on my side of the bed when I moved," she said. "I don't want you to think I was snooping." She placed the poster on the coffee table in front of her, face down. "What are you going to do?"

"Me?" I asked, startled.

"Yeah," she said, simply. "What are you going to do about this?"

"I want to get rid of it," I said, the words leaving my mouth faster than I could understand them.

We crept outside barefoot. The wind upset the pinwheels in the front lawn, making them shudder and clack behind us as we walked toward the water. The ocean churning against itself muted the sound of my own breath.

I flinched as my feet touched the water, but we kept walking until the ocean licked up our thighs. Violet guided the poster beneath the water and held it there. She said we had to keep it there until we saw it dissolve, so we could be sure that the ocean wouldn't try to bring it back to us.

The ocean doused the paper thin, tearing off corners, making the letters blur into each other. When the waves tried to swallow big strips, Violet pulled them back and crushed them in her pale hand, rinsing the pieces off her fingertips back into the water to feed the ocean slowly.

I watched the water eat away at a girl I never asked to be. It felt like a funeral, or a ritual, and for a second I let myself believe in something other than what could leave its mark on me. Bruise me, bleach me, cut me open. Here I was, bathed in salt but with no open wounds.

A thrill ran through me, and I ducked beneath the water and came back up sputtering, laughter tearing from my throat. Violet laughed with me, and as the last of the paper melted in the water, she bent her head down into the ocean like a heron. She whipped her head back, her hair splattered and dripping down the back of her dress like milk.

We stayed to bask in the black water, rippled in the distance with moonlight. We knew the air would slice through our wet bodies when we stepped out, chill us and send us home shivering, but in the ocean we were waterlogged, too steady and steeped in giddiness to be moved. It was possible my parents would still find me, but in that moment the idea that they would give up seemed so much warmer. They would throw away all the pictures they had of me and start over. Yes! They would have another child, a good daughter who knew how to stay on land and could smell a storm before it came. A daughter who didn't try to get rid of herself. A daughter faithful to their word, grateful for the clear future they rolled out before her. Yes. That idea was so much warmer.

Valerie

BEFORE VALERIE'S HELP, I had never had an orgasm with another person. I only knew how to finish myself off with other objects, never my own hand. I could alchemize household objects into pleasure with some baby oil and plastic wrap—a vibrating toothbrush, a cucumber, a bedsheet tied into knots and then stuffed under my bed until I could wash out my sweat and desire by hand in the bathtub when no one was home.

My own hand only ever left me hopeless and sticky. So, despite the fact that I had only ever found other girls worth looking at, I convinced myself I was straight. All my straight friends told me they had faked it with their boyfriends before, so I felt okay doing the same thing with mine. To me, the most exciting part about having sex with boys was faking it. I liked the process of preparing for sex, setting the stage. Pressing the hair on my head flat, culling all the other hair from my body, spending an hour on my makeup—lip gloss, sparkling eyeshadow, powder that absorbed all oil and light. My cue was their hips falling out of rhythm, their voice hitching, their breath steaming clouds from the sweat that dripped from their foreheads in between my breasts. I was only ever asked once if I was faking it, when I tried to be demure, natural. They believed me more when I gripped their sheets in my hand and twisted them like leashes, when I bruised their pelvis with my bucking, when my screams summoned all the dogs in the neighborhood to chorus.

Then I met a girl named Pauly, the only other Black girl at the lesbian bar. I had only gone in hopes of feeling like the prettiest person in the room. When I was little my mother taught me how to scope out the outline of a place and the people who would be there so that when you arrived you could be the most beautiful person there. *You want to look put together*, she'd say, and I would picture my limbs unstitching from my body if I was caught outside with pilled-up socks. Before birthday parties, I'd sit in my underclothes in the back seat while she walked in first to see what the kids were wearing. She'd play like she was just dropping off the gifts and then rush back to dress me in one of four outfits she had planned for me—depending on how well the other kids were dressed. When I was looking for a job at the mall, I only applied to stores with girls who weren't prettier than me. *Pretty girls feed off your ugliness and turn it into a virtue for themselves*, my mother told me. *She'll plant herself to you like a weed and only be beautiful by comparison. That's why the most gorgeous women are all married to ugly men.*

I thought it would be easy to be the prettiest girl in a lesbian bar. I assumed if someone saw me, they'd think I was in the wrong place. I wanted to make an island of myself—I wanted to feel good about not succumbing to something that threatened to engulf me. *Not today*, I could think. *Today I am dry, granular, slipping through a clenched fist.*

But I couldn't look away from the lesbians in the bar that night. I had just turned my last boyfriend loose and went out looking to feel better than someone. I couldn't feel superior when every girl I passed sparked against my skin and reduced me to shadow. I think it was my newfound lonely, a shroud that had been haunting my body for a month, that made all my thrashing and screaming in some boy's bed hollow out my chest. It made me want to grab at any girl who looked at me and press their hands to my chest, have them beat on it and see if the noise came back eating itself. Pauly grabbed my hand after spilling her drink on my dress, leading me to a stack of napkins and tipsily wiping at my shoulders. I stilled her hand at the seep on my dress, and she asked if she could kiss me, and then the only thing I could hear was her pulse in my mouth.

When we first fucked, I expected to be overwhelmed with pleasure. I expected her touch to wear down whatever barrier my ex-boyfriends couldn't—I wanted to be waterlogged in her warmth and salt. But those things never came, and I reached a point when my own expectant little moaning echoed in a silent room, with only the sound of my slick body as a lonely applause. I thought that lesbians were supposed to touch each other's bodies and already know the reflection of themselves. I thought I was supposed to be touched by a woman and have her fingers latch in me like a key. But instead, I revved up my breath and pretended again.

It's not like I didn't desire her. Pauly was a butch with a continuous grin and no filter, which manifested as her leaning in my ear the night we met and telling me that I was the prettiest girl in the room. She occupied her body with an ease I worried might have been normal for everyone except me. She sat in her body as if she was the only one who ever had to look at it. She demonstrated how she had learned to piss standing up by parting her pussy like a curtain and pulling back with her fingers like the reins of a wagon. She took her top off on her balcony and stayed there until the sun browned her as dark as her nipples. She'd curl her body around my back at night, her warm belly flesh against my spine, her breathing deep and steady. During these moments, when my own breath curdled in my throat, stifled and paced, I realized I didn't know the natural rhythm of my own breathing. I only knew how to imitate.

When we walked down the street together my focus orbited around where Pauly latched herself to me. Not only because I wasn't used to how people's glances garlanded from me to Pauly to her hand around my waist, but because I found myself suddenly preoccupied with what she saw when she looked at me. Before we'd go out together, I'd stand alone in front of my bathroom mirror, memorizing the way I looked when I held my face in specific ways.

With everyone else I had been with, it always felt like there was a clear correlation between the way I dressed or the way I did my makeup or how I styled my hair and their interest in me—I could direct what they did with the movements of my own body. With Pauly, I could never track any difference between the way I presented myself to her and the way she treated me. She ran her fingers along my knuckles as she whispered stories to me about shooting wild pigs with her brothers in Arkansas. She planned picnic and museum dates and gave me her jacket when I had dressed too skimpily for the cold. She held my gaze so patiently and so sincerely when I spoke to her, I wanted to scratch my eyes out.

VALERIE

I faked my orgasms with Pauly for three months before I started searching the internet for: *why cant I cum? how to have orgasm? if i cant cum does that mean i dont like her? if i can't cum does that mean i dont like her lesbians?* until my eyes cured from the salt and light.

During all this searching, I discovered an email in my spam folder with the subject line, *SEXOSPIRITUAL HEALING: BREAK THE SHACKLES ON YOUR BODY*. The body of the email read: *Valerie, professional sex expert, trained in curing sexual curses! Valerie! offers tarot readings, crystalized bodily rejuvenation, yonic transformations. First consultation is free with the purchase of a tea or book. See results in less than a month!*

And then an address.

I wasn't planning on actually going, but I drove by on my way from work, just to see. The address led to a rubbly parking lot that sat across from a gas station with half the lights blown out from its canopy. There were a few restaurants, a beauty supply store, a nail salon. Above the nail salon, a staircase led to an office building. Rust gilded the railing, and the paint peeled off the body of the building in pink citrus rinds. The sticker letters on the glass panels of the door were all chipped and flaked away, so I couldn't make out whatever the office had been before. When I crept inside, the door creaked shut behind me and the room choked away all the air. Only thin gusts lapped at my ankles, slithering through the spaces in the floorboard. There were dim salt lamps plugged in in different corners of the room, set on the floor and warming the room pink like a mouth. Hefty bookshelves lined the wall, reaching toward the crowded ceiling. Strings of crystals, dozens of dreamcatchers laced with dust, paper garlands bellying toward the ground scribbled with different handwriting—their shadows stretched across the walls. A woman sat on the floor in the center of the room with her eyes closed and her hands splayed open on her knees like dead spiders.

I shuffled my feet in front of her, unsure if she was asleep or meditating. She breathed as slowly and deeply as a bear. As I watched her I found my own breathing growing heavier, slipping in line with hers, until her eyes cracked open and she quickly rose in front of me, towering so high, her head nearly brushed the ceiling.

Her clothes tented her body and her red hair reached down her back, frayed and wild like rope ends. She smelled like mildew and dried sweat, and I turned my head to suppress a gag.

"Welcome," she said. And she spread her arms out wide to gesture to the bare room. "Are you here for sexual wellness?"

I told her about the email and tried to tell her what was wrong without actually saying it. But she stopped me in the middle of my stammering and leading and traced her hand along the top of my head, only the heat of her skin touching me.

"Oh, girl," she said, "you've got the worst case of it I've ever seen."

"It?"

"All your desire is tamped down," she said, "like hair in the shower drain." She brought her hand down to caress the top of my head, and I only moved back when I heard myself shiver.

She unzipped her coat only to reveal another underneath. She kept unzipping and unbuttoning, peeling back layers of fabric like petals as she dug through her pockets. She pulled out stones and pamphlets and bundles of herbs and then put them back. Each fabric layer released a new wave of some heavy odor—Callery pear trees, gingko leaves, ocean backwash. Until she reached some layer close to the softness of her body and handed me a cloudy bag of some chopped leaf.

She told me to steep the leaves and drink the tea I made from them every morning, and the second I got home I threw it in the garbage. I was determined to never look at it and never think of the woman above the nail salon ever again, but I gave in that next day, after that night when Pauly came over and I contorted my body on the couch, pretending to choke on my breath again. I watched as Pauly wiped her slick and her sweat away with a paper towel, watched her weight shift as she sighed with pleasure. She offered me a napkin to do the same, and I wiped it along my body, sighing from an exhaustion I didn't exert. She tossed them into the trash can, and that next morning, I moved the stiff napkins aside to grab the bag of leaves and make myself a cup of tea.

Every morning I chugged the bitter drink down, ignoring the heat scorching my throat. The aftertaste was the worst of it; after the heat had subsided and numbed my tongue for the day, I was left with the sense of something stale, a film netting the back of my throat that only revived itself every time I swallowed. I couldn't wash it out no matter how much I gargled mouthwash and scrubbed my mouth and chewed gum. Besides this, the only effect of the tea seemed to be that for the rest of the day after I drank it,

I couldn't shake a certain heat from my skin. I stood under the air vent and laid my head in the freezer, but the warmth swelled in my face, rising but never bursting.

I was constantly sticky with sweat. Any makeup I wore slipped from my face and was replaced by the flush blooming under my skin. The sweat seeped into my eyes and gave me the appearance of constant weeping. I left copies of my legs on coffee shop seats, and when I woke up next to Pauly on the nights when she slept over, I looked down at the outline of my own sprawling body. My body smoldered away all my energy. I dragged my salt-burdened back through the day, and when Pauly kissed my neck or sucked at the sweat pooled between my breasts, my body leaned heavy against hers. I couldn't bring myself to summon tension in my stomach when she touched me, so I just lay there on her bed—soaked, simmering, and numb.

Am I doing something wrong? she asked me.

And I was afraid to tell her that I was just bad at being sincere. I didn't want her to question what other parts of me were fake because I didn't think I could come up with an answer for her. So I said, *I'm tired. I'm just tired.* And when she pried, I said, *Jesus Christ I'm just tired, am I allowed to be tired sometimes?*

I stood next to Pauly and felt my wet hand drowning a moat between us. At gay bars, at work, during artsy little lesbian gatherings, I looked around the room and thought, *I am the nastiest bitch here.*

I stopped drinking the tea, thinking I'd rather be a fake bitch than a sweaty bitch with no girlfriend—but the burn persisted. It festered my head dizzy, made my limbs swell until they were sore to the touch. I spent hours sitting on

VALERIE

the bathtub floor, willing my skin to temper under cold water, and instead feeling the warm runoff fall down the drain.

After a shift at work where I stood behind the counter with my head bent over, sweat dripping from my nose while I rung up small-sized bikini tops, I drove to the rubbly parking lot. Most of the stores were already closed. There were only a few cars scattered in the lot. The store signs ignited the colors from oil puddles. Valerie's dark storefront sat shadowed above the nail salon.

A distant sound of sloshing grew louder as I crept up the staircase. I peered through the window, but Valerie's soft heartbeat-pink lamps weren't strong enough to reveal anything but her outline, hunched in the center of the room.

The doorknob lingered against my palm, sticky with something I couldn't see in the darkness. Valerie's paper garlands hung loose from the ceiling, the ends curling against the ground like snakes, alongside most of her dreamcatchers—the strings torn loose and the feathered ends tangled. The contents of her bookshelves were left in disarray, all the books turned onto their sides, splayed flat on the pages, or perched on their corners, a frantic and senseless reorganization.

As I walked closer to her crouched, shaking figure, my foot brushed up against something that rolled across the floor. I scrambled for my phone and shone the light on the ground to reveal a slushy cup from the gas station across the street. They were scattered all across the room—empty slushy cups, the insides pooling with the melted dredges of red syrup.

For a moment, with the light on her, I assumed I wasn't looking at Valerie. She sat among a collection of striped cups. All her layers had been sloughed to the ground around her. Her arms and neck were scrawny, as if her skin was just thin film over bone. Her belly was soft, rounded where her stomach met with her legs, which were thick and strong, the muscles in them pulsing as Valerie balanced on her knees, head tipped back as she poured a slushy into her open mouth.

She was soaked in sweat. It made a circlet on her forehead and plastered her red hair to her face. It rolled down her back and gathered in the folds of her stomach, it dipped from her legs and led to a shining puddle beneath her.

Valerie finished a cup, knocking it against her teeth to collect the last drops, then throwing it across the room. She snatched up another and began to guzzle it down. The red slipped into her mouth and dribbled down her chin, and when it landed on her skin, small plumes of smoke coiled into the air. I was suddenly more aware of my own heat, how it whip-cracked along my joints. My phone slipped from my hands as I lurched toward her, snatching the cup from her hands and tipping it into my own mouth—waiting for relief.

Instead, the heat of my mouth curdled the drink to caramel, bubbling hot in the back of my throat. My knees gave out beneath me as I retched up sugar shards while smoke fumed from my throat. My groans echoed in my ears as I rested my head against the floor. The floor creaked. I saw Valerie's feet step toward me—then felt both her hands on my back. I knew there was heat on her skin too, but between our two bodies her touch was cool.

VALERIE

I didn't even mind her smell, which had been heightened by sweat and heat. I bridged my body into her touch and let her slip my sweat-heavy shirt up so she could place her fingers on my skin. I sighed and tried to savor the bit of relief I felt. I glanced up at her. The dazed look in her eye from when I first met her was gone. She seemed more tethered to earth, less erratic and strange now that I could see her body and she wasn't something hidden. Her breath was steady, she looked calm and worldly above me suddenly, like the way adults seem when you're a child. She looked down at me in pity.

A sick feeling twisted in my stomach. I pulled away and shot up to stand over her and struck her across the face. Her body twisted easily under my hand. I didn't look long enough to see her hit the ground. I turned and ran down the steps, peeling burnt sugar from my mouth. I sped home with all my windows down, trying to gather a wind that could chill me. I wanted my roiling body to be churned to vapor, cast out and only left as a whisper against some girl's turned cheek. I didn't know what to do with my body when it wanted. I only knew how to smother and scream in place of desire.

When I got out of my car and my key wouldn't fit in the building's lock, I realized I had driven to Pauly's apartment. I cursed and crashed my fists against the door, flinching the moment my raging echoed back to me. I stood in the circle of the porch light and listened to how heavy the quiet smothered the night: no crickets, no frogs, no cars rumbling down the street, just my own frantic breathing. I took a step to walk back to my car before the lock clicked.

Pauly stood doused in yellow light, dressed for sleep,

the peaks of her body showing through her slouching clothes. I turned toward her, my hands rising to brush her collarbone, the outline of her nipple, her hipbone—I had never let myself linger on the small parts that made her.

She said my name, and I needed her to say it again. So I kissed her. I pulled my name from her mouth as my hands searched for more small miracles that made up her body, striking my desire against her body. When she came up for air her mouth was red—more than kiss blushed. She looked down at me like she had never seen me before.

I wanted to ask if it was okay that I wanted her this badly, if it was okay that my desire was spinning my body into light, if it was okay that I leaned on her, all my heat leaking onto her.

I could only ask if I could spend the night.

When I came, all the strings I used to posture myself into something beautiful were singed. I sprawled my body across her bedsheets and used them to wipe my sweat, I let the steam huff from my throat, and any noise I made was lost to the sound of my heartbeat in my ears. All the unbearable heat from my body slipped into something heavy and bright in my belly as I rode out against her mouth. When I came, I smiled in relief.

The heat in my body had broken, my next breath was cool. I looked at Pauly. Everywhere her body had curved against mine was tinged with heat. She stared at me, as if searching for something, and I let her look. We slept face to face, passing one breath back and forth between our mouths.

In the morning, all my clothes were sweat and slushy stained. I rested my lips on Pauly's shoulder to check the temperature of her skin, and before I could get up Pauly twined her arms around my stomach, trying to keep me there. I could feel her skin sticking my dried sweat, I could smell myself as I lifted my arms to curl around her neck. I laughed as she nipped at my neck, and I built up the strength to tell her I had to go, that I'd be back.

I drove back to Valerie's shop, assuming I owed her an apology for hitting her. But when I pulled up, the parking lot was blocked off by fire trucks and police cars, their lights blinking dimly in the morning sun.

Valerie's shop had burned to ash. The staircase had fallen from the building, and it lay discarded on its side, half burned. Black smoke snaked up from the charred remains, but the building below seemed untouched.

A woman stood across the street, leaning against her car and drinking a tallboy Red Bull. I started toward her and then hesitated. I realized what I must have looked like—shirt crunchy with sweat, makeup still smudged around the eyes. This woman was glossy. Mascara done up to her eyebrows, clothes crisp, shimmering nails clicking against the can. I glanced at my own hands—acrylics grown out, one nail snapped off at the tip. She looked up at me before I could turn away.

"Excuse me," I said, "do you know what happened here?"

The woman sucked her teeth and gestured to the cop cars.

"I've been waiting for an hour now to get into my own salon," she said. "It was already all burned away by the time anyone got here. I'm supposed to open in thirty."

She sighed.

"What about the woman up there?" I asked.

She glanced at me sideways. "There was someone there?"

Oh. I stepped as close as I could to the wreckage as I could to peer over what was left of Valerie's store. All her garlands had burned away, but I saw the last remains of a bookshelf. I thought I could see the gleam of her stones and crystals through the carpet of ash in the parking lot, shimmering like new wounds.

The wind picked up and carried some of the ash toward me, and I sputtered as it stuck to my mouth. Some stray bits of book pages floated past the police cars like confetti and landed at my feet. I looked down to try and see which small words had not been obscured by soot and burnt edges. Along with these, I watched a clump of rust-colored hair curl and catch along the curb. It quivered like a leaf stuck with all the other debris, then broke loose and flitted out of sight like an ember.

Swallow Worlds

AMANDA PUTS POWDER on my jawline and makes my face look slimmer. This is good because lately when I look in the mirror I can't tell if I'm skinny or fat. This feels final in a way. I was fat, probably, and now I look skinny—at least in the face. She lengthens the ends of my eyebrows into daggers. She colors in my lips with waxy liner and thick gloss, then wipes the excess with her pinky finger. I could cry. I want to tell her to do it again, to keep her finger there and count the beat of my pulse.

She moves onto my eyes, but when she tries to put eyeliner on me, I can't stop twitching and blinking, smearing cold black paint on my eyelid. She clicks her teeth. *Girl*. She's smiling. I let myself cry, and she's had enough.

She makes me lay my head in her lap, looking up at her. It only slightly helps. "I feel like I'm in middle school," I say.

"But middle school girls are all great at makeup now. You see them all over the internet looking like twenty-something year-olds. All of thirteen."

Amanda is on the internet a lot. I'm not. The last time I had a phone that let me online, I spent eight straight hours reading the hate comments about celebrities I liked and had a panic attack for a week. Amanda gets those comments under pictures she posts of herself trying on different makeup and clothes. They're flawless—the clothes always intentionally scanty in some way. Her nipples poking through a sheer shirt, the skin of her tummy peeking over shorts, exposed thigh blooming from the slit of a pleated skirt.

I asked her if she made the photos intentionally sexy. She made fun of me and asked if I thought she was sexy. Then she said, *What's sexy? Nipples?*

In the context of the rest of the body— I began.

She cut me off. *I don't want any context. I just want my nipples to be my nipples without someone trying to force meaning in that.*

She told me that when she got boobs in the fourth grade, boys would pinch and poke her chest, as if trying to burst her skin open. When she told her auntie, she told Amanda to stop being fast and cover up, but her mom wouldn't buy her a bra until middle school because she thought a nine-year-old having a bra was too grown up.

Amanda had tried to explain to her white-girl friends at school.

Fast? they asked. *Like quick?*

She thought about it.

Slutty, I guess. But what was *slutty* anyway? She had looked the word up online and found porn. "The first time I saw it I felt like throwing up. Not because they were naked or anything, but because all the women looked like they were being killed or something."

I understood what she was talking about. Women in porn weren't just fucked, they were drilled and screwed and pounded, gaped open and left to swallow. The idea appealed to me—to be manipulated into a placid thing. Something that didn't feel any desire to buck away what wanted to pierce it. But I couldn't say that to Amanda now. What would she think of me?

So we both walked to the park in fitted T-shirts and no bras. We sat in the field, surrounded by grass and white mothers who saw our nipples from across the field like they were targets. Brown trampolines to bounce their eyes between. Amanda just leaned back and let her nipples be nipples while I conjured a bunch of images from her body—mountains, knives, my own budding heart I could pinch between my teeth. I covered mine and tried not to look at hers.

Amanda is a god. She's absorbed so much of the internet. I think she knows everything. Whenever we meet up she tells me about everything that people were angry about that day and laughs; she recounts tragedies from across the world and shrugs. But even though she knows so much I still find myself wanting to say I think she's wrong. So when she tells me about the middle schoolers and their makeup I ask her if she's being serious. She goes through her phone and shows me pages of reedy-voiced little girls drawing new eyes, new lips. Recording themselves opening boxes and boxes of expensive makeup.

"See?" she says. And I think about this little girl who goes to the same middle school I used to go to. She's skinny with straightened hair that puffs up at the roots and swoops across her pimply forehead. She dresses in band T-shirts from Hot Topic and leggings that bunch up at her ankles. I volunteer at the library, and I see her alternate between doing her homework and looking up random things on the internet like *what's beneath horse hooves* and *vintage playboy magazine covers.*

I think about her, then I think of a different girl in middle school from only eight years ago. Eight years ago feels like a long time until I break it up into two spans of four years—and then I'm not sure if I'm old or young. I thought this girl was a god because she wore acrylics and purple-tinted lip balm and wore shorts that showed the crease of her ass. Her eyelashes were long, thick, and stuck together in black clumps. But I had never seen a girl my age who was allowed to wear so much makeup. I asked her if she had any mascara on. She said no. Lied straight to my face and made me think she came out of the womb with sticky eyelashes that brushed her eyebrows.

Instead of explaining this to Amanda, I just say alright and let her make me up like her—shiny and slick. Being in her lap is enough to make me feel like I'm being made into something untouchable. In middle school, I'd go down these internet rabbit holes that began with me searching for information for a history paper and ended with me watching grainy videos of men being stoned to death or burned alive, or animals being struck in the head with metal pipes until their faces turned to mush. Amanda holds my head steady, nails poised against my temple and chin, holding my twitchy head in place.

She lets me up and tries to tell me how I can make myself up like an untouchable god myself. When she leaves I spend the night dancing in the mirror and stopping to stare at my own face. I think: *I could open my slick mouth and swallow the world.*

I try to make myself up the next day for work, but I can't figure out how to flick my eyeliner the way Amanda did. Instead I smear the remainder of what's left after I wash my face—smudgy and black around the eyes. I just look tired. But I put on lip gloss, in hopes that it looks like I did it on purpose.

I spend the whole day at the library worrying the edge of my lip with my finger and then reapplying lip gloss I just wiped off, doing it again—before just taking it off completely.

That frumpy girl with the crispy hair keeps looking at me from behind the computer in the corner, and I can't help thinking that I did too much, putting on a skin that doesn't fit me.

She stays until closing, and I have to tell her it's time to log off. The screen blurs her face with light. She is so close to the monitor, it looks as if she plans to crawl inside it. She doesn't see me until I stand right beside her. She startles when she notices me but can't click away before I see that she's watching porn. I pull a face, less because of the girl and more so because I'm shocked; we don't have the site blocked. But later on, I feel guilty because she probably thinks I'm looking at her in disgust.

"We're closing now," I tell her.

She nods, her eyes rimmed red.

I hope she knows I wasn't looking at her in disgust. I come up with different realities in my mind and ponder over which was better: That she forgets about this in a week or two. That she takes my reaction and uses it to hate herself. Or that she'll just be embarrassed for a few days and then move on and avoid me, only for the memory to ghost and ache in her chest whenever she thinks about her body and how it fits next to someone else's.

I tell Amanda about the worlds I made up the next time I'm at her house.

She shakes her head. "Do you even know this girl's name? You're thinking too much. Forget about it."

So I let her thumb open my mouth and varnish me in glitter, letting all my worries ease back down my throat—letting them sink in my belly and weigh me down.

Better Days

WHEN JORDAN WAS a baby, I couldn't put her down. She looked so much like me. My nose, my bushy eyebrows, the curve of my lip. She felt like a mirror I pulled from my body. There was no one else around I could measure her features against, so when I held her, she was just all my sharp edges. I obsessed over my own image and licked my thumb to smooth down her stray brows.

I raised her the way I would have liked to have been raised—a slicked-down life. Thumbed numb and dull. Every morning we got up at six and tapped on the same loafers, had the same breakfast (one egg, two sausages, and toast), and she came back from school to play cards and let me brush down her unruly hair with coconut oil.

She's twelve when she tells me the world is going to end. She's twelve, but she still comes to my door first thing in the morning. She crawls from the end of the bed, lies on her back, and presses her shoulder into mine. I assume it's a joke, or something to do with schoolwork, so I ask, "How is the world going to end?"

"In two months," she says, "the sky will turn pink, and the earth will split like an egg. One half will explode and the other will continue into an ice age."

"I don't understand."

"I saw it in a dream."

And I'm further confused. We usually share the same

dreams. She would tell me that she dreamt about being locked in a room surrounded by the sound of echoing footsteps that grew closer and closer but never came, and I tell her that it must have been me trying to get to her because I had dreamt of running down a hall toward a door I could never reach. Or she would tell me that she dreamt of falling slowly, and I would tell her that I dreamt of looking up and seeing her, but instead of falling she was floating up.

I haven't thought about the world ending since Jordan was born. All my catastrophes are pre-Jordan, and I suddenly fear they've been transferred to her somehow. No one had told me about all the things a baby inherits from you.

I try to tell her what no one ever told me. I say that the first time I felt like the world was ending, I was eight and my dad left. His body left, but so many of his things were still there. Coats, pointy brown shoes, a watch, a ring, cologne, soap, a half pack of Newports. I gathered some of his things when no one was watching and put them on in the garage—the only place I could be alone. My legs stuck to the cold cement floor while I sat in the light of a foggy hanging bulb, swallowed by my dad's coat, his watch slung against my wrist, unlit cigarette in my mouth. I'd curl against myself and breathe these in, cupping my own face with his sleeves to imagine he was there.

When my mother caught me, she gathered all his things, piled them high on the front lawn, and had me and all my older sisters watch as it burned. I only managed to save the cigarettes.

The fire left a dead circle in our grass that never grew

back, and the taste of it smoldered in my mouth for so long after, I thought it was my father as a ghost trying to wrap his hands around my throat for not doing more to keep him there.

But the world didn't crack and collapse, I tell Jordan. I try to smile and be encouraging.

Jordan shakes her head and leaves the room.

I try to keep things as normal as possible. She's getting to be that age—the doom circling her head will pass. Except, for the next few weeks, she begins to drift away, her shadow unhinging itself from mine.

She stays out after school later than I'm used to, first by minutes, then by hours—the yawning expanse of time like a held breath. When she is home, she won't play cards with me. She sits on the ground in silence while I fix her hair, combing out the knots at the nape of her neck. She stops coming to my room in the morning, and if I don't get up before her she leaves without eating.

The days flip like tossed coins, one day clear, the next gray, until they begin to shift in and out of each other, one arriving before the other can end. The sun beams from a clear sky while the rain sizzles against a softening black street. The ocean licks closer to the shore, and each day the television lists out the names of those who can't keep from walking in. The bodies are dragged back out, and they line the sand in rows—as if they're being used to count out the days.

I do my best to keep things normal. I wake up early to make breakfast, I buy cute rain boots, a pair for each of us. I place sandbags along my door to keep the water from seeping inside. I make Jordan take an umbrella to school and insist on driving her—after I catch her on the roof one night, eyes waterlogged with the ocean.

Her face is thinner. I can't remember the last time I looked at my own face, so I don't know how much of myself I'm looking at.

I tell her the second time I thought the world was ending was 9/11. I never lived in New York, but I watched the towers smoke and buckle on the television—the first like a bad knee, the second as if the ground had called for it to come back. I sat on my knees, breath fogging the television for hours, while my mother made frantic calls to my father. I didn't know she still had his number. Suddenly the ghost was back. Fire swarmed in my lungs, and I watched the smoke on television race through the streets and assumed that someone was angry at me, that I had done something wrong and this was the cost I had to pay.

But you don't have to feel that way, I tell her. *You don't have to carry the world on your shoulders. It's not your responsibility. You're doing great*, I say.

She looks at me, her face sharp. *I know*. Then she leaves.

Then the girls come, following her into her room. I recognize the first few from our conversations—Sydney, Coco, Lindsay—but the rest file in faster than I can learn their names. Jordan says they're just friends from school and nothing more, so I know them only as girl with red hair, girl with freckles, pale girl, short girl, girl with a black birthmark on her cheek.

Jordan and her girls travel in packs, moving in rotations, orbiting around her. They send Jordan walls of texts with hearts and sparkles and rainbows. When they're in my house they speak almost exclusively in whispers. Their voices slip into one the same way the water from the rain and the water from a neighbor's running hose and the water from the tears I wipe from my face all rush to converge at the bottom of the slope of the neighborhood. Until they break into laughter and they're just girls again.

At the beginning of the second month, Jordan doesn't come home, and after four hours of calling and getting no answer, I drive out to find her.

She is on a cliff that peaks above the ocean, even more so lately, with how tightly the water clings to land. A line of girls around her age, some that I've seen and some who are complete strangers, crowd at the base of the cliff and make a single file to the top, where Jordan sits. They drop off gifts and trinkets around her: cans of apple soda, packs of playing cards, matchboxes, pliers, hammers, ice picks, press-on nails, frayed denim skirts, matted fur coats, house plants in pots, sparkly lip gloss, soup cans, socks, butterfly knives, sandbags, and a pink sparkling dress draped across her lap. The items sprawl around her and stack behind her, with only one thin path leading to her feet.

I cut past all the girls and kneel in front of Jordan. The ocean air makes her hair curl like broken violin strings.

"You have to come home," I say.

Jordan says she can't. "I have to be here when the world ends." Then she looks up at me, her dark eyes bright. "Stay with me."

And I want to. My daughter hasn't smiled at me like this in so long. I want to sit cross-legged next to her, ask her how to play this game, but she looks so different. I've looked into the mirror and found something etched into the glass. My only instinct is to bash the reflection with my fist in hopes I can rearrange the shards into something else.

I yell at her. "I don't know where this is coming from, you're being overdramatic, and if you don't get in the car right now—"

I pause, my hands fisted at my sides. I've never had to punish her outside of time-outs when she was little, littler, and she is already mimicking that expression she used to make—eyes closed, face screwed tight—when she was tucked quiet into a corner.

I leave, and some of the girls call me names as I pass. Mostly about being old or a bitch. I feel heavy and slow and not nearly as much of the bitch I used to be.

She stays there until the end of the month, even while people walk into the ocean around her, even after all the girls have gone. I bring her food and water. Bowls of stew, turkey sandwiches. When I boil beans I can usually turn down the fire under the pot before it overflows, but now I forget about them until they catch up to me—hissing and frothing over, stubbing the fire and staining the stove black.

I come up to her at night with her dinner. I never see her eat, but the bowls I leave her are empty and the spoons are dirty. I pack those up and leave the new meal at her feet. Her eyes stay shut, as if sleeping, even as I clink utensils and brush against her knee. The dress is still in her lap, shimmering in the moonlight like a big, pale fish.

I sit next to her and tuck my head into my drawn-up knees. I tell her, *The third time I thought the world was ending I was at my senior prom.*

I used to be a girl who was most easily tracked down by asking who I had spent the night before with. Maybe it was a phase or maybe it wasn't, I wouldn't know, because since then my greatest obsession has been molding my own reflection into something I can bear looking at. But I used to be a girl too sharp and bright to hold for long: a peak boys reached to say they did and a star girls kissed only to tongue the burn in shame later.

I liked the secrecy of girls, how none of them could muster the courage to talk about me, even though their whispers still swam in my ears. Kissing girls felt like catching a ghost I could see, could touch. A ghost I haunted, not the other way around.

Boys were different. They didn't keep anything secret. They called out my name in the street and in the school hall like they were trying to summon something within me—some dirty vision for themselves. I liked to pretend with them. It gave me a break from being myself, when I could split my body open and do my best impression of their desire.

I went to my senior prom wrapped in a pink dress. I didn't have a date, but I made a game of seeing how long I could pull girls away from theirs. I spent the dance tucked in corners or crouched in the bathroom stalls with my head up someone's dress, counting the seconds by heartbeat.

I left before most of the kids could spill out of the dance hall. It was getting to be that time, when the king and queen had already been given their shiny plastic crowns, and the DJ steadily inserted more slow songs into his playlist, and all that was left of the dessert table was an anemic collection of plastic cutlery, a sputtering chocolate fountain, and a handful of soggy strawberries. Only the kids who lavished in the idea that their prom was their last chance for youthful happiness slumped against each other and shuffled their feet in the confetti until a parent chaperone had to tell them it was time to go. I wanted to end my good time before someone else ended it for me.

I kept my father's cigarettes in the glove box of my car. They were stale by then, and I was down to my last few. I only smoked one once a year. Since I had gotten my car, I smoked as I drove down the street with the windows down, so the smell wouldn't stick to me as much. The stench of it stayed out of my car and off my body for the most part, but the evidence of it would stay on my fingers until the next day.

There were hardly any streetlights in this place I used to call home, just long, crumbling roads surrounded by grass and fences. For a while it looked like I was the only one on the road, until I saw the body of a dust-colored pickup flash underneath a streetlight behind me before slipping back into the dark. They didn't have their headlights on, and I kept watch behind me as we passed another streetlight, and the glaring faces of some boys from my school stared back at me. I only knew them by their girlfriends.

I didn't want to drive home and bring a car of angry boys to my mom and sisters, so I turned down long roads that didn't lead to my house and tried to keep myself from shaking. The cars multiplied and stretched out behind me like a parade, glittering in the streetlights that only came every few minutes. The boys hung out the windows, hollering and throwing things at the back of my car—bottles, cans, corsages. They kept a steady, menacing pace. I flinched when they lurched forward, stomping on the gas and veering onto roads I had never gone down. The cigarette stuck to my dry mouth, ash dusting my lap as I huffed in the smoke.

I don't know if they lost track of me or if they just decided to leave me alone, but by the time I let myself stop driving, the sun was up and I was in a different state. I hung my head between my legs and threw up on the floor of my car. I wiped it up with tissues from a gas station, and I never went back home.

When I open my eyes, Jordan is staring. We are both crying. The water laps at the edge of the cliff and the dress crinkles in her lap as she leans over to kiss me on the cheek. I leave for the night.

IN THE MORNING, the world starts to end, and I am late to the chaos. The television beeps, like someone laying on a dial tone, and then static. My windows are broken—the glass shimmers across the ground, crunches beneath my heels. Outside, the sun shines so brightly, edges and form seep into one glowing expanse of white. For a moment, I'm left squinting at the sound of rushing water and the crunch of metal as cars slip and crush together. When my eyes adjust, the trees are all bare and the grass is dead, thin and yellow beneath a bubbling pool of rushing water. The sun swells in a pink sky, but the air is biting cold.

The street is too crowded for my car, so I stumble barefoot uphill, against the water. My robe and slippers sop behind me, heavy and tugging, so I let them go, and they dissolve in the street like tissue paper.

I'm sweating and shivering when I reach the cliff. It sticks out of the churning water like a hand grasping upward. The girls crowd toward the top, their faces flushed pink, and I can't tell if it's a reflection of the sky, or if they're cold, or if it's because they're smiling—staring up at Jordan on the peak. She's in the shimmering dress, and her hair curls wildly around her head.

I try to call out to her, but I sputter and choke on salt water, slipping as the ground begins to rumble and a crack churns the waves and echoes in the air. I can't tell just yet which side of the egg I'm on, and panic grips at my chest. I don't know which side is better to be on—the one frozen in suffering or the one with a definite end.

The clouds in the sky warp, spinning in a haze, and the cliff seems to recede farther and farther. I beat the water with my fist, less trying to swim and more trying to get Jordan's attention. A numb roaring sound hums in the air. Jordan turns. She's too far for me to see what her face looks like as she spots me, but I do see her dress gleam as it catches the sun, and I see her raise her hand and wave back to me.

I wave to her until her figure is swallowed by light as she and the other girls turn into shimmering scales on the body of the hill. My arm is raw and red where it beat the water, and my legs are heavy. I let myself stay still, and as the shining cliff warms my face, I cannot tell who is falling and who is rising.

A Matter of Survival

KITTY HAD TO get fake teeth in the fifth grade after I punched her in the mouth for calling me a monkey. She had danced around in front of me, hooting and scratching her armpits, because the way I sat squat on the blacktop to read made me look like an ape. I grabbed her twisting blond pigtails and yanked her mouth to my fist like my mother had talked about doing to a girl in a parking lot once when I was still a peach pit in her belly. Kitty's two front teeth skittered across the ground like dice, and the blood leaked from her mouth as steady as a faucet.

I collected the teeth and kept them in a sewing box. From then on, any fight I got into, even if I lost, I made sure to collect something. Fistfuls of hair. Scraps of shredded clothing. A pink acrylic nail that had been lodged into my arm.

My mother was mostly upset about how I came back home with my clothes streaked with blood and dirt. She was still dressing me well into high school, in pleated knee-length skirts and stiff frilled blouses with white collars that crawled up my neck. My hair greased back into a tight bun. I went to school with rich white kids whose socks always stayed glaringly white, no matter how many times they stretched out on their backs under the bleachers, spelling each other's names in spit on their bellies.

My mother bought me secondhand clothes with the

quarters from her teeth. Shining silver coins leaking from a hollowed slit in her mouth. My first memory is of me sitting propped on the counter of a Goodwill while my mother searched through stacks of clothes her friends had hidden behind the counter, thumbing through the least frayed and pilled dresses and jamming her thumb into her gums to make the coins spill past her lips like a slot machine.

Her teeth were just one of many places she kept her money: closed in carved-out books, taped inside a cowskin drum, tucked in the toes of rain boots. Before company came, she would instruct me to move the money—swollen plastic baggies of quarters and rubber-band rolls of cash— to new hiding spots, and would tell me to do it again once company left. Once, she saw a five-dollar bill fluttering out of my jacket pocket. She snatched it from me, and her grip cut into my shoulders. *I could beat you*, she said. Breath iron sharp. *I won't because I love you, but I could.*

My mother always wanted me to be grateful for things she didn't do to me. Like when I met Kitty again in my senior year of high school in a swimming pool parking lot. She stood leaning against her car, barefoot in a bikini top and shorts. Her long blond pigtails had been chopped and buzzed close to her head—not nearly enough to grasp in a fistful. Two shining chili peppers bobbed from her ears, dripping water onto her shoulders.

We stared at each other until her eyes felt like hot stones against my skin. I told her she looked like a genuine dyke. She flashed a grin that showed all her teeth. I shuddered. I had expected to hurt her.

In the back seat of her car, I kept desperately trying to grab onto her hair while she rutted in my lap and tore open my collar to drink the sweat flooding in the hollow of my throat. My hands slipped against her buzzed head and fell to grip at her waist. My tongue grazed her top teeth. I thought maybe I could feel how the front two might have been smoother than the rest, and I felt that because I had the real thing I had already conquered her body. I wanted to pluck the fake ones out and crawl into the empty space to live there, rot her gums black. Or had a bunch of dentists shoved metal in her mouth to screw in her porcelain teeth? If so, I wanted to wear it down with my spit until it rusted, and she could think of me when ruddy saliva oozed from her mouth.

Kitty gave me a ride home, and my mother watched me shamble out of her car with my shirt untucked and one of Kitty's shining chili peppers tucked into my fist.

I could move you back to Oklahoma, she cried, and we both understood this as a kind of death sentence. *You'll be stalking those fields until you dig a rut for yourself to be buried in*. I told her that sometimes it felt like I was drowning on land. I told her that sometimes I walked the two hours out to the beach and stood on the edge of the pier until I felt sea-salt air corrode the strength in my knees.

She laughed. *If only you had grown up like me*. A story I had heard three times by then, about how my grandmother, Grandma Junebug, made my mother sit outside on the porch if she wasn't home by the time she'd been told to be home at. If she left the porch, my grandmother kept the door locked for longer. One time, my mother amassed three days on the porch, licking up food in bowls my grandmother had pushed out the front door for her and watching the sun shiver the horizon. Another time, she had tried to force her way through the window with her elbow, and Grandma Junebug sent her back out, leaving my mother to pick bloody shards of glass from her arm alone.

My mother did not send me to Oklahoma permanently, but she decided to send me there for spring break, after the rising threat of girls in bikini tops skating through the streets outside our house—like chlorine-soaked packs of gods—plucked her nerves as the ground turned brittle beneath their wheels.

My Grandma Junebug: a woman whose skin stretched over her body like a thin billowing sheet. Bird wrists, downturned eyes. But her voice rose from her chest like a howling wind in a hollowed-out cave, the strength of the sound proving there was life from the source it came from. She spoke constantly—labyrinthine chatter that exposed the personal lives of neighbors and churchwomen. The point of conversation always seemed ten steps removed from its origin, and in the midst of her dizzying narrative she would put her hand around my wrist to invite me to laugh at her own joke, and I'd notice just how strong her grip was and how straight she kept her back while mine listed against the weight of an hour or two passed. But she'd still be talking, eyes glinting and focused on me. *And do you want to hear what happened next?*

When Grandma Junebug asked for something, she demanded it.

My mother thought I might learn some womanly traits from Junebug—or at the very least I would be forced to copy them for a couple weeks—but the extent of any forced femininity stopped after Junebug took both my hands in her fierce grip, observed my short nails, and asked me if I wanted a manicure. She chose the color, a milky nursery pink. Then she brought me to bingo. Where one of the tubes of pink ink cracked and spilled down the front of my sundress, and I absorbed a room's worth of cigarette smoke until she won. Later, Grandma Junebug asked me if I wanted to accompany her on her afternoon walks, at the hottest point of the day when the red dirt we kicked up mixed with my sweat-drenched blouses and made them blush.

Grandma Junebug asked me if I wanted to go stargazing. She had her hand rested on a pistol in her nightgown pocket—as if she planned to shoot the stars loose from the sky, which seeped into the ground and finally made the red clay black. We could hardly see in front of us and instead had to rely on the shrinking dot of light from the porch and the sounds we made between ourselves. Junebug's slippers slapping against her heels. Metal clicking against her thigh. The steady shuffle of grass broken by a flinching body that made me gasp and that Junebug confirmed to be some sort of threat. She swiped her gun from her hip and shot at the spasming thing. I took my phone from my pocket. We were both marked with sparkling confetti droplets of blood from the jackrabbit twitching in the weak stream of cellphone light.

We took the rabbit home. I carried it swaddled in my jacket like a baby, my finger plugged in the seeping wound in its neck. Junebug said rabbits were a good source of meat. Of course she wouldn't eat it, she told me, but she knew a white woman who shot and killed them all the time for her and her two kids. We would give it to them as a gift in the morning. I followed her voice without looking up, too busy watching the stars stream by in the jackrabbit's still eyes.

The kitchen light seemed eerily bright after traipsing outside all moon-eyed. I caught a glimpse of myself in the hallway mirror as we made our way into the kitchen. Oversized souvenir shirt blooming red at the chest, legs crusted with dirt and blood, sweat glowing across my forehead. Some distorted Virgin Mary.

Junebug snatched the rabbit from my arms and set it flat on the kitchen counter, took the same knife she used to cut the skin off apples, and jabbed it into the rabbit's side. She stuck her fingers into the new wound and tore back the skin with two hands, as easy as if she were peeling away a coat.

I learned how to do this after my husband left, she said, *just in case he came back.*

I had never met Junebug's husband. I had only heard the stories my mother told about her father, Johnny, a man who stood as a light beam for my mother when she was so anxious about my future, she could only stand to look back. *My father*, she would tell me, *was the kindest man I'll ever meet. He provided for me the way I do for you*, she would say, relentlessly. *No matter how poor we were, he brought me gifts: lockets on gold chains, slick black Mary Janes, miles of glittering ribbons for my hair.*

I had come to like this man simply because of how my mother only seemed to smile when she spoke of him.

Junebug's steady wrinkled hands twisted the head off the rabbit's skinned body—exposed crystalline muscle—her mouth a grim rut.

She told me how she remembered him.

A MATTER OF SURVIVAL

They first met on a dance floor, where she—dripped out in pale yellow, hair a frothing halo around her head—shimmied her way toward a man dressed in white who shook his hips at her like his dick was a fishing line.

The first thing Junebug noticed about him were his hands, curved delicately and gently cupped like a child's, as if he had never done anything with them. When he gripped her body against his crotch, his nails dug into her hips so hard, four curved moons bloomed into her sides and still shone there today. *I had never felt so desperately wanted before*, she said.

Instead of asking if she would marry him, Johnny said, *Baby, I've got to have you.*

Their favorite thing to do was dance along to Junebug's record player. They swayed long after the music fizzled out, sweat sticking their bodies together in the summer. Junebug liked that Johnny wanted all of her—the salt building on her skin, the scent of her. He kissed her as if he worshipped every tooth in her mouth.

When she couldn't dance with him, Johnny's body moved in other ways. He ate all the food in her fridge and grew upward until the seams of his suit popped and his neck arched against the ceiling. The hair on his chest thickened and rolled down his shoulders and back, thick and black like the raised hackles of a dog.

He brought other women to Junebug's home and left imprints of their bodies in her couch—their perfume and sweat embedded in the threads of her furniture. When she tried to shoo him away, like she would any dog, he turned and latched his teeth into her neck, snapping bone. She crawled into the bathroom and pressed bath towels against her wound until her shallow breathing solidified into a whistle. The mis-healed bone stuck out against the skin of her throat, like a hand through a curtain.

When her belly swelled she thought lying on her stomach or hanging upside down or throwing herself down the stairs might capsize the pit in her stomach—but the baby stayed. When their daughter was born, small and pale, she fit neatly in the center of Johnny's palm, like a pearl.

Junebug had been raised believing in God and therefore could not kill herself like she wanted. So she played dead instead, curled on her bedroom floor, feeling the fabric of her dress catch air against her steadily shrinking body. Junebug said she thought she played dead too well. Houseflies crawled against the surface of her eyes, the smell of her body filled the air, her daughter gurgled in the next room—but she didn't move. There were moments during shallow inhales that she thought she had finally died, but the whistling from her cracked throat reminded her of the movement beneath her skin.

Johnny liked new and beautiful things, and his daughter was new and beautiful. He doted over her and came home every morning with necklaces and lace fabric strung between his teeth. Bruised flowers and ticking watches. He held them over her when she was a baby and watched her fat fists reach for whatever he dangled, and when she was old enough to go to school he sent her off in fur coats and diamonds tinged pink from whatever woman he had bit them off of.

Johnny did not cook for her; instead their daughter lapped up drips from left-behind bottles, sucked on the hems of tulle skirts, and gnawed on pearl necklaces to slurp down the strings. Her hunger swelled, and the weight of jewelry anchored her weary body. She cried out for days, constant and drilling like a siren. For Junebug, the noise meshed together with her teapot throat and the humming beneath the floor. Johnny frantically tried to quiet their daughter with more shining things. He dropped dangling earrings down her open mouth only for her to swallow and spit them back up, deboned of their jewels. Necklaces swirled and choked up her neck like horseshoe rings, wringing out the cries in her neck to a pitch. Junebug said she heard Johnny then, whining and circling the floor in a frenzy, his dog ears sore.

Then, the sound of ringing metal and a last choked-off cry that she recognized only because of how similar it sounded to her own. She carried herself to that echo and saw their daughter on the ground in a heap of coins, all sprouting from her red-coated mouth like a fountain. Johnny shadowed over her—chest heaving, fist raised.

He turned to Junebug with his head bent, and she told me that she used to be able to tell where the man ended and the canine began, with Johnny. As if she were sectioning him off for cuts of meat, keeping the man (his childlike hands, the way he danced) and doing away with the dog (his loose dick, his bite). Maybe her eyes were still cloudy from all that time spent wishing she was dead, but she could not unstitch a man from a shadow. There was no use pretending a dog was not a dog.

She stumbled up to him, tripped into his body, and latched her dull teeth into the give of his shoulder. He howled and swung, trying to buck her off his body, but she hung onto him like a parasite, tearing away chunks of his skin until his arm hung loose from its socket, bone stark white against black fur.

When he flung her to the ground and her legs buckled beneath her, she did not stay down. She crawled after him with blood and fur in her teeth, chasing him out the front door—hobbling on three legs instead of running on two.

I used my stained shirt to help wipe the countertop clean and threw it in the garbage with the other stray limbs and rabbit skin. Grandma Junebug held my hands, her grip as fierce as the dead. I didn't know how she saw herself. If things are just what they were, was she still dead? A ghost watchful over her porch steps. And what the hell was I?

I think it's better for you to mess around with girls anyway, she said. *You'll have an easier time beating one when she tries to kill you.*

When I came back home, I shook all my fight prizes loose from their box and tucked Kitty's loose teeth and earring into an envelope. I told my mother where I was going and who I was going to see. She wrung her hands, fighting the urge to quell whatever desire she thought she saw in me with her fists. I told her again. I wanted her to get used to me wanting more than the coins from her teeth.

In the pool parking lot, I tucked Kitty's envelope in her windshield, and I felt her coming toward me as I walked away, the skin on my neck sticking up, remembering her. She called out to me. I felt the same weakness in myself when I stood above the ocean, wondering how far I would have to fall to feel something that stuck around longer than the urge to die. Instead of turning to her, I let my body ache with that want, letting it settle in my joints and carry me to something else that could satisfy me.

Previous Publications

Sympathy for Wild Girls was originally published in *Lunch Ticket*, issue 17, June 2020.

Thinning was originally published in *Prose Online*, August 2022.

Pollen was originally published in *Brushfire Literature and Arts Journal*, volume 72, issue 2, May 2020.

Nico and the Boys was originally published in *Free State Review*, issue 12, February 2020.

Butterfruit was originally published in *Cleaning Up Glitter*, volume 2, issue 1, March 2020.

Better Days was originally published in *SORTES*, issue 9, March 2022.

A Matter of Survival was originally published in *SORTES*, issue 7, September 2021.

Acknowledgments

Thank you first and foremost to my agent Ismita Hussain, my trusted guide and true believer.

Thank you to everyone at Feminist Press, including Kameel Mir, for bringing clarity and patience. Thank you to Rachel Page and Jill Twist for their copyediting knowledge.

Thank you to Nick Bernal of Burn All Books, and Jeremy Tenenbaum of *SORTES*: for housing words I've written and being the first to offer support upon first hearing about the publication of this collection.

Thank you to those I've met at San Diego State University, including Rema Shbaita, Warren Stoddard, Joey Rougas, Megan Sigwalt, Robert Lang, Alex Blum, and Jessica Aram, for their enthusiasm, support, and friendship. The work you all do energizes me and makes me want to be a better writer. Thank you to Matt de la Peña and Stephen Paul Martin for your insight.

Thank you to Emily, my oldest and most trusted friend. Thank you to your family as well, for their kindness.

Thank you to my mother and grandmother, Jo and Sue. Matriarchs of my small family.

A heaping thanks to Garrett Aja, Rhiannon Scray, and Aidan Tojino for your friendship and care. Thank you to Star, Sophie, and Robyn for all your laughter and late-night talking.

And thank you to Sejal, my love.

Demree McGhee earned her BA from the University of California San Diego and her MFA from San Diego State University. Her work has been published in *Lunch Ticket*, *Wax Nine Journal*, *Prose Online*, and more. *Sympathy for Wild Girls* is her debut short story collection. She lives in San Diego, CA.

The Feminist Press publishes books that ignite movements and social transformation. Celebrating our legacy, we lift up insurgent and marginalized voices from around the world to build a more just future.

See our complete list of books at
feministpress.org